# One Sycamore Sunday

## STACEY WEEKS

CHASED BY GRACE
CHANGED BY LOVE

Grace and Love Publishing

Cover image from Unsplash: freestocks-yB2TGLr-rVo-unsplash.jpg

ISBN 978-1-7387413-2-8

Grace and Love Publishing

# Free Short Story
## Download at StaceyWeeks.com

When sweet peppers and jalapeño mix,
anything can happen.

Addison avoids visiting the city. He hates the
crowds, traffic, and pace. He especially hates the
compact vehicle the rental company insists he'd
reserved. But then he runs into Sarah. Or, more
accurately, she runs into him, mixing sweet
peppers and jalapeño with burnt metal, petrol,
hot pavement, and her desperation to not merely
survive life in the city but find a place to thrive.
Addison isn't looking for a weekend thrill or a
romantic entanglement anymore than she is.
They both want to go home. Maybe, together,
they'll find their way.

# Praise for The Sycamore Standoff

Weeks is a writer I count on for sweet contempo-
rary romances with faith messages to make me
think. Sycamore Standoff combines sympathetic
characters with heartening takeaways about the
freedom of living in grace and the power of
community.

— AUTHOR EMILY CONRAD

The town of Sycamore Hill is warm and welcoming. The heart of God shines throughout the
story. I really enjoyed The Sycamore Stand Off.

— JULIA - BOOK REVIEWER,
CHRISTIAN BOOKAHOLIC

One of the things I enjoy about Stacey Weeks' writing is her ability to present a powerful & touching gospel message organic to the story, without it feeling forced or preachy. Instead of stopping an entertaining story for a sermon, Weeks uses the faith-centered elements to enhance the characters' journeys on the page and point to the Source of peace, strength, and courage.

— CARRIE ~ BOOK REVIEWER,
READING IS MY SUPERPOWER

# More Fiction by Stacey Weeks

## SYCAMORE HILL

To Sweet Beginnings in Sycamore Hill

The Sycamore Standoff

His Sycamore Sweetheart

The Sycamore Slopes

One Sycamore Sunday

A Sycamore Secret

## MISTLETOE MEADOWS

Mistletoe Melody

Mistletoe Mission

Mistletoe Movie Star

*Mistletoe Meadows Anthology

(contains all three Mistletoe titles)

## STAND ALONE TITLES

Fatal Homecoming

The Builder's Reluctant Bride

In Too Deep

*To God, who has done far more for me than I could ask for or imagine.*

*So, whether you eat or drink, or whatever you do, do all to the glory of God.*

*1 Corinthians 10:31*

# Contents

# CHAPTER 1

# 8:30 a.m.

"Oliver!" Kim Jansen tapped her booted foot on the hardwood floor at the bottom of the short staircase. If he didn't hurry, they'd be late for church again. A crash and a thud sounded from inside his bedroom.

"I coming." His closed door muffled his reply.

Oliver was probably looking for something that he *just couldn't live without.* Her three-year-old came by his flair for the dramatic honestly. His father, Hayden, had always been a showman.

Bitterness filled her mouth, as it always did when she thought of Hayden. Kim swallowed the sourness and tightened her grip on the banister. Hayden wouldn't interfere again because Jackson, his twin brother, made sure of it.

The identical brothers shared the same rugged good looks, blond, wavy hair, and piercing blue eyes, but that's

1

where the likeness stopped. Jackson was as good as Hayden was evil, proven when Jackson sacrificed his relationship with his twin to bring Oliver home. For that, she'd be forever in his debt.

But he didn't do it for her. He did it for Oliver.

She pressed two hands against her midsection as her insides flip-flopped. At least, that's what she told herself.

"Oli-verrrr!" Forced cheerfulness softened her tone. There had to be some sort of brother code that forbade a guy from dating his twin's ex.

Oliver's bedroom door opened. His soft curls bounced as he descended the stairs, dragging his stuffed bunny behind him. She'd given him the toy last month for his birthday, and he hadn't let go of it since. The rabbit's head thumped on each step.

"I coming."

When he reached the bottom, he stopped in front of her and lifted his face. She bent and kissed his cheek. "We need to motor, my little love." She ruffled his hair, her caress softening the urgency of her words. So, they arrived late for church. It was a small thing. When Oliver was gone, she would have given a lifetime of last-to-arrive-at-church-Sundays to have her son back.

She shook loose the sad memories of their time apart. Hayden stole everything from her when he took Oliver, but letting her mind linger on that season of her life only birthed bitterness. And bitterness about the parental abduction that separated her from Oliver for fourteen months never led her to a good spiritual place.

Sucking in a breath through her nose, she lifted her chin. She'd forgiven Hayden, and she firmly believed the Lord would enable her to act accordingly despite his unrepentant heart. But forgiveness wasn't the same as reconciliation. Grabbing her purse, she slung it over her shoulder, refusing to let guilt take root. She'd chosen to forgive, for her spiritual health, and had since discovered that forgiveness was more than a decision. The process took time.

"Do you have everything for Sunday school?"

Oliver attached the Velcro of his shoes and beamed at her. The sneakers were on the wrong feet. She should probably tell him to put on boots, but the fact he wore footwear at all was a win worth celebrating.

"Ready!" Oliver lifted his arms for her to pick him up.

"Not quite, buddy. You need a jacket." She handed him his puffy orange winter coat. The February chill had dropped below normal temperatures for their region, and their friendly groundhog had announced six more weeks of cold.

She helped his arms into his jacket and zipped up the front, ignoring the way he swatted her fingers because he wanted to do it himself. He wedged his bunny into his armpit and tugged on mittens and a hat.

The wind swirled the dusty snow and stung their cheeks as they trudged to the car. Frigid air made it hurt to breathe, and the cold seemed to make the scent of pine from the trees that lined the property stronger. It only took another five minutes to get Oliver buckled into his car seat and start toward the church. Eight-thirty. Not too bad.

She turned on the Christian radio station and hummed along to a familiar tune about God's goodness. Oliver chattered to himself. He held the bunny up to the window. "See Unca Jackson?"

"We'll see him at church."

"No working?"

"Not today."

Jackson worked for the Ontario Provincial Police, who provided a presence in Sycamore Hill. He worked every other Sunday, which meant either Constable Stuart James or Constable Noah Brown patrolled today. Kim still had to pinch herself to believe that Jackson had upended his career to move to Sycamore Hill to be part of Oliver's life.

The wind iced the fog as the tail end of nasty, blizzard-like conditions swirled. Forecasters predicted it would be clear by midday, in time for the Winter Carnival. Every year, the same travelling carnival set up camp on the outskirts of town. For one week each February, child-friendly tunes played on an endless loop, attracting children like sprinkles to a sugar cookie. At least the music didn't play on Sunday mornings.

"Rides?" Oliver cranked his neck as they passed the fairgrounds.

"Maybe after church." She'd ordered three tickets

online last week, but she knew better than to tell Oliver about it this early in the day. He'd pester her all morning.

A small SUV emerged from the haziness behind her. It crept closer, so she tapped her brakes. Her stomach heaved at the lack of traction. The snow must have pressed into ice. She tapped her brakes again, but the guy didn't take the hint. He rode her backside like they were hitched. Clenching her jaw, she squinted in the rearview mirror. She didn't recognize the man and couldn't read his license plate, not that it would help. It wasn't like she could report him to Jackson for following too closely.

She flicked her gaze back to the road in front of her. Brake lights. She slammed the brake pedal. The wheels slid, and the antilock system kicked in and pumped the brakes. The back end swung left, then right. She cranked the steering wheel the opposite way. The arch got bigger and bigger as she tried to steer them out.

"Mommy!"

The vehicle spun three-hundred and sixty degrees and skidded across the center line. "No, no, no, no, no!"

By some minor miracle, there was no oncoming traffic. She stood on the brakes. The back tires spun as the front tires turned. When they finally gripped the road, she yanked left as hard as she could. She avoided hitting the vehicle that had stopped in front of her, but the car shuddered as they hit the ditch. Loose snow absorbed their arrival.

*Oliver!* She twisted.

Eyes spread wide. Pale skin. Bunny clutched in his fisted hand. But he was in one piece. *Thank you, Lord*.

"We're okay, honey." She rubbed his knee. A hum vibrated in her ears. She exhaled, and inch by inch, the tightness in her neck and shoulders lessened. They were okay.

A giant tear slid down Oliver's cheek.

They needed to get out.

The ditch wasn't deep, but the overnight snowfall had filled it. There was no way she'd be able to open Oliver's passenger side door, but she could open hers.

The other drivers had stopped, and three men hurried toward her. She forced herself to inhale slowly and deeply. They were okay, too.

"Are you all right?" The men reached the car and huddled around the driver's door.

"We're fine. Are you okay?" They appeared unharmed. She unbuckled and retrieved her purse, which had slid to the floor on the passenger side. "I'll call the police—"

The door jerked open, and her rescuer snatched her phone from her hands. Before she could speak, the man tossed it into the snowbank.

"What are you doing?" Wind stung her cheeks, and incomprehension blurred the edges of her vision. She thought the other men might intervene. But instead, they wrenched open the back door and fumbled with Oliver's buckles. Her mind denied what was unfolding. This wasn't real. It couldn't be real. Her ears roared.

"Mommy!"

Shock transformed into panic. She lunged toward Oliver, slapping the men's hands away. A growl erupted from deep within her. She'd kill them to protect her son.

A sharp pain split her cheek. The acrid tang of blood. What was happening? All she could see, smell, and hear was Oliver's fear. Her fear.

"Mommy!"

Cloudiness took over. Another blow landed, and it flung her into the passenger seat. Then came the sound of heavy feet and shouting.

Terror laced Oliver's words. "Don't hurt my mommy!"

She only caught bits and pieces. Oliver flailing his arms and legs. A rip. A wail. They pulled him from the car. She fought for consciousness. Oliver's cries were the only sounds that penetrated the roar in her ears.

The men were bigger and stronger. An angry bark emitted from one, and Oliver's wails faded. Kim struggled to right herself. She blinked rapidly but still couldn't see straight. Her cheek stung. Her body ached. She was wedged in a seat, her breathing shallow. Her heart beat in her forehead. The car was too quiet. It was a screaming silence that filled her mind and exploded from her lips.

And the radio played as if everything right in the world hadn't gone wrong. The artist crooned about a good God.

Kim fumbled with the door handle. Her panicked hands refused to work. Finally, she gave up and pounded the glass. "You're not good. You're not a good God. Not a good Father!" She pressed her forehead to the glass and wept. A keening. *Not again*. Hayden wouldn't do this to her. God wouldn't let it happen.

But Hayden had done it before, and God didn't stop it.

*She had to think of Oliver.*

Her mind cleared. She blinked. The hum of a thousand caffeinated drinks shot through her body. The passenger door wedged into the snowbank. That was why she couldn't open it. She clawed her way to the driver's side and out. A blast of cold hit like the arctic winter. Her boots sank into the snow past her ankles. Was Oliver on foot? He only wore shoes.

She should have made him wear his boots. Why didn't she insist?

She scrambled up the snowbank, her hands and knees burning with cold. Blowing snow filled the tracks from where the two SUVs had driven away. Minutes. Only a few minutes had passed.

They were gone. Oliver was gone.

Her legs gave way. *No.* Pushing herself up, she steadied her trembling arms. She needed to fight.

"Oliver!" A crawl morphed into a run. She sprinted toward a dark spot on the white bank. If she didn't stop moving, she'd find them. The toe of her boot jammed into an icy lip, and she lurched forward. Cold shot up her arms as her hands tunneled through the snow.

Oliver's bunny. A torn terrycloth ear dangled by threads. She clutched it against her chest. "Oliver!"

# CHAPTER 2

# 8:45 a.m.

J ackson McGregor made all the appropriate sounds as he listened to his twin brother recap his latest adventure. He waved at Pastor Owen and Gloria as they crossed the foyer, pointing at the cell phone against his ear as the reason he didn't say good morning.

Owen nodded and pressed a hand to the small of Gloria's back. She was talking about flowers, her large gestures indicating these weren't just any flowers. The couple was probably discussing their wedding, which was only three months away.

Their friend group seemed to celebrate one engagement after the other lately. First, Eli and Meg. After a short spring engagement, they married in December. Owen and Gloria got engaged in September, and Ben and Emma right before Eli and Meg's wedding. It was like wedding fever had taken over the young adults. If the pattern held, Kathryn and Ethan would be next.

The pattern would skip him. He'd have to be satisfied with being Kim's friend and Oliver's uncle. A guy didn't marry his brother's ex. Not a good guy, anyway.

He glanced at his watch. The church service started in fifteen minutes. Kim should be here by now. Several families milled about, hanging up coats or swapping winter boots for inside shoes. He should be helping Oliver out of his winter gear, not chatting with his brother.

"I got another call. Can you wait a sec?" Jackson put his brother on hold to pick up Kim's call. "Did Oliver make you late again?"

"I need you." Ragged, short sentences. Clipped words. Heavy breathing.

Playfulness evaporated. He dug in the front pocket of his jeans for his car keys. "Where are you?"

"I'm on—" She sniffed with a snort-cry.

Pastor Owen paused at the side door that led to his office, and turned to look back at Jackson. His brows pulled together with a concerning look.

He mouthed to Owen. *Kim's in trouble.*

Kim would be on one of three roads. She'd stick to the plowed ones. He clutched his keys in his fist and scrunched his face, pressing his fist to his forehead. "Holiday Drive? Main? Sylvester? What road are you on?"

Pause, then a deep sucking sound. "Accident." Kim drew in another noisy breath. "Men. He's gone. Oliver's gone."

An acute sharpness tore through him. Men? Oliver? "Where are you?"

Owen's gaze followed Jackson. Curiosity colored Gloria's face. Jackson's hurried movements drew the attention of several families.

Meg and Eli approached. "Everything okay?"

Jackson shook his head, too focused on Kim to answer Eli.

"Oliver's gone. Gone." Each word from Kim came out shriller than the previous one.

"Kim! Where are you?" He needed a location, and he needed it now.

"H-H-H-oli-day Drive."

"I'm on my way."

Jackson bolted to the coat rack and grabbed his jacket from a hanger as he clicked back to Hayden. He'd only recently reconnected with his brother. Guilt had driven him to seek him out. For months, Jackson had fooled himself into believing the time he spent with Kim had just proved he was a good uncle. An invested family member. But somewhere, along the way, he'd fallen in love.

Even though Kim wasn't his to claim.

Sure, she and Hayden had never married, but they had a baby together. A child that deserved a mother and father. But Oliver would have no hope that they might reconcile if his uncle swooped in and captured his mother's heart.

"Keep us posted. We'll be praying!" Pastor Owen's

words slipped out the church doors as they began to close behind Jackson.

The cold slapped Jackson's face as he raised the phone to his ear again. He ground his molars and pain shot down his jaw. Had Hayden sensed Jackson's feelings for Kim? Was this a pre-emptive strike? "What did you do?"

"Is everything okay?"

No, it wasn't. And Hayden had lost the right to ask years ago when he whisked Oliver overseas without Kim's consent, leaving the mess for Jackson to clean up.

"What's wrong?" Jackson could hear the familiar sound of knuckles popping in the background. Hayden's nervous response to stress.

"What did you do?"

"Nothing."

"Hayden—"

"Look, man. I'm not even there. Whatever happened, it's not on me."

Jackson unlocked his car and got in. He wasn't buying it. "Where's Oliver?" Impatience oozed through clenched teeth.

"Oliver's missing?" Hayden's pitch rose. Clear panic, but was it genuine?

"I don't have any details yet." Jackson's Bluetooth kicked in as he threw the vehicle in reverse and roared out of the parking lot. He wished he had the cruiser so he could light it up, sirens and everything. Jackson drummed his fingers on the steering wheel. If Oliver was really kidnapped, he'd have to call his Staff Sergeant.

"I'm on my way," Hayden said.

"Don't." Jackson wasn't sure he could trust him. Besides, Hayden lost any claim he had on Oliver years ago. He might sing a song of repentance regarding how he'd mistreated Kim, but that didn't mean he meant it. The guy was a chameleon. He became whoever he needed to get what he wanted. And right now, Jackson didn't have time to figure out Hayden's real agenda. He hung up on his brother. An officer could track Hayden down later and question him.

He redialed Kim. If she ditched the car, she could have lost consciousness. Did Oliver get out? Maybe he went for help? If they were lucky, the boy was knocking on some kind stranger's door, and the responsible adult would soon ring the police to report it.

But he wasn't banking Oliver's life on good luck. Or a kind stranger.

Kim picked up immediately. She sounded more in control. "What if this was Hayden?"

Jackson slowed for an intersection, looked both ways, and sped through. In less than a minute, he turned onto Holiday Drive. "Let's not make any leaps. I'm almost there."

"Hurry."

That was it. One word. One loaded, raw, painful request. "I am, Kim. I am."

She couldn't muffle her cries.

A rock lodged in his throat. Could Hayden be involved? Abductions by strangers made up less than one percent of kidnapped victims. Parents took ninety percent. Ninety-nine percent of kidnapped children returned alive. He clung to the statistics. He didn't want to it be Hayden, but if it was Hayden, at least he wouldn't hurt Oliver.

"I'm almost there." His knuckles whitened, and his fingertips tingled. He loosened his grip on the steering wheel. Would his brother do something like this? Was it fate that he was on the phone with Hayden or was that Hayden securing an alibi? He could have hired someone. Was this backlash for Jackson falling in love with Kim? What kind of man did that?

The kind who had done it before.

Jackson spied Kim's vehicle, and his chest lurched. "I'm here."

The back end of Kim's vehicle stuck from the snowbank. She stood to the side, shivering, and pressing her phone to her ear, hugging her body. When they locked eyes, heat surged through him. He pulled over and thrust the car into park.

Kim didn't wait for him to come to her. She barreled toward him with a guttural wail and threw herself into his arms.

Pressing his face into her hair, he inhaled her soft floral scent. He consoled her, but only for a minute. They didn't have the luxury of time for grief. Every second counted.

He eased her to arms' length so he could see her. Really see her. A laceration on her cheek wept red on her sweaty skin. Her hair, usually straight and smooth, was ratted and tangled. His temples and ears pounded. His vision tunneled. She was hurt. A faint shadowing darkened underneath her watery eyes. It promised to be a pretty shade of purple by tomorrow. Her gray complexion seemed more pale than usual against her dark hair. Almost translucent. Shock was setting in. He needed to get her warmed up.

He steeled himself. She needed a cop, not coddling. Get the facts. Make a plan. Treat it like any regular case.

Except it wasn't. It was Oliver.

He moved her slowly and deliberately toward the passenger side of the car. "Tell me everything that happened."

Kim's words wobbled. "A car riding my bumper distracted me."

"A car? What kind of car?"

"Not a car," she corrected. "A sport utility vehicle." Her exhalation shuddered. She sounded more confident. "It was definitely a SUV, and it was black."

"Okay, so this guy rides your tail. Then what?"

"I didn't see the other SUV in front of me. It was too late."

"A second one? Were they travelling together?"

"They took him, Jackson. They took him!" She pinched her waist and bent over, trying to suck in oxygen. "Right from the back seat. I tried to stop them. He hit me—"

His stomach clenched. He twisted her back into his arms and held tightly, squeezing his eyes closed. *Lord, please. Please.* It was all he had.

He opened the car door and helped Kim into the front passenger seat. "I need to call Emma."

Emma was the only medical professional in town. The nurse practitioner filled in as a paramedic several times in the past.

She fought his hands. "I don't care about me!" Her violent response momentarily stunned him. "They took Oliver!"

His gut cemented. This was bad. Really bad. "I'll call Stuart. He's working today. And my Staff Sergeant. We're going to need help."

She nodded, tears soaking her face and dripping onto the burgundy scarf tucked into her coat collar. "Find him."

It killed him to have to turn away from her. Every cell in his body wanted to hold her and never let go, but he had to detach. It was their best chance.

He made several quick phone calls. Sycamore Hill wasn't equipped to deal with a kidnapping. He stumbled over the word, *kidnapped*. Just thinking about it made his stomach heave.

"Put out a BOLO notification to local police departments. I'll arrange for the detective and Missing Persons unit, the negotiator, and the IT officer." Every word Jackson's Staff said added a rock to Jackson's gut. This was real. Oliver was missing. "Stay with Kim until the team arrives."

"Yes, sir." They'd have to peel him off Kim if they tried to order him away.

Next, Jackson called Constable Stuart James, the on-duty OPP, and updated him.

"I'll get started on authorization for an Amber Alert," Stuart said. "I'll call in Noah, too."

Jackson finally called Emma. When they disconnected, Jackson didn't immediately turn around. He pinched his eyes shut. He was nowhere near clear-headed enough to do this. *Help me, Lord. I need to focus.*

Jackson knew the statistics. Of the one percent of stranger abductions, forty percent of the children died at the hands of their abductor. The first three hours were the most important.

*Help me compartmentalize. Help me gather evidence so the team can hit the ground running when they get here. Don't let me feel anything. Please, oh please, God, please, lead me to Oliver in time.*

He didn't say any of that to Kim. Statistics wouldn't help her. Letting her see his struggle to focus wouldn't help her. Only answers would. He turned and crouched in front of her. She sat in the vehicle, half in and half out, holding her head in her hands. He tentatively brushed his fingertips across her shoulder.

Her head jerked up. The skin around her red eyes bunched, and she fisted her hands.

"Let's warm you up. I asked Emma to bring Ben with her. He'll get your car to the garage. Give me your keys. I'll leave them under the mat." Emma had only recently returned to full-time work at her clinic, having just recovered from a serious shoulder injury.

Jackson despised needing to be so matter-of-fact. His stomach soured and threatened to expel his breakfast, but he swallowed it. He had to detach. He had to work the steps. It was the only thing keeping his head clear. Otherwise, he wouldn't have the mental strength to do what needed to be done. Oliver was counting on him. It'd been fifteen minutes since Kim called him. Thirty since the abduction. That left two and a half hours before they crossed a line that he wasn't willing to cross.

*Please, Lord.*

Kim nodded numbly and handed over her keys.

Emma wanted to know if she could share what happened with the church family.

Kim's heartbeat pulsed in her neck. She nodded permission, and he reached over her to crank the heat and reposition the vents to blow on her. He retrieved an emergency blanket from his trunk and wrapped it around her. He grabbed a water bottle from a case he kept in the back, twisted the lid off, and gave it to her. "Drink this." He fired off a quick text to get the prayer chain moving.

She took it, but didn't lift it to her lips. She stared vacantly at the set of tire tracks disappearing in the snow. Catatonic.

She needed him, but Oliver needed him more.

He forced eye contact. "I'm going over there." He pointed to her car in the ditch. "I need to look around."

She nodded, eyes glazed. She tugged the blanket tighter and rocked. Then the whimpering started.

He made himself walk away. He needed to work the case. He also needed to hold her and tell her he was going to find Oliver and bring him home. But he couldn't do both. Not by himself. And she needed him to be a cop more than a comforter. She just didn't know it. Finding Oliver was all that mattered.

Another phone call assured him the wheels were in motion. His Staff would get as many officers from nearby detachments as he could. Stuart was tracking Hayden down and sending local officers to pick him up, and Noah lived ten minutes out of town. He'd be there soon. Jackson crouched to study the tracks in the snow. It had stopped snowing, but the roads were a mess. It'd take Noah twenty to thirty minutes to get here. The Missing Persons unit was even further out. Two to three hours. Oliver didn't have that much time.

The harsh wind erased the crime scene and threatened to hold up their reinforcements. But if snowdrifts blocked the routes in, then they also blocked the roads out. That meant Oliver was still here.

*Lord, please.*

Oliver. His nephew. The son of the woman he loved.

CHAPTER 3

## *9:15 a.m.*

K im paced the short hallway in her house, sloshing hot coffee over her hand. The burn failed to register, but she felt the liquid drizzle over her wrist. She wiped the back of her hand on her thigh, and the spill absorbed into the denim. After changing from her church clothes into jeans and a sweater, she pulled her hair into a short ponytail. She numbly went through the motions of making coffee and putting out cream and sugar for Jackson and Stuart. It felt normal. How could life continue in its usual way when her son was missing? The world kept rotating and orbiting the sun when everything should have stopped. The universe should pause as they waited for news.

Any news.

Good news.

*Please, Lord, bring good news.*

Jackson was across her living room, leaning over

Stuart's chair. They'd sent her to gather photographs of Oliver so they'd be ready for the Missing Persons unit coming from Orillia. Jackson had been avoiding her since they'd returned to her house. It was evident in the small things, like how he evaded her gaze and kept a room between them. He was pulling away, and the rejection pierced her soul.

Neither Jackson or Stuart looked up as she sighed. Kim sagged against a doorjamb, clutching her most recent picture of Oliver, running one fingertip over the image of Oliver's face. Over and over and over again.

Had she misjudged Jackson? If she couldn't count on him to be by her side at a time like this— Why wasn't he holding her? Why wasn't he promising everything would be okay? With Oliver's bunny wedged between her forearm and chest, she pushed through the doorway and set the photographs on the table. Jackson never looked up. She squeezed the bunny tighter. Since they returned to the house, she hadn't put the toy down. The idea of putting it down felt like admitting that Oliver was gone. It made little sense, but her heart accepted the flawed logic, even if her mind couldn't. She fingered the rabbit's torn ear. She needed to find her sewing kit. The rip would upset Oliver.

She yanked out the drawer in the end table. No sewing supplies. She moved to the bureau, opening and closing random drawers and cabinet doors. With each failure to secure her sewing kit, her heart wound tighter.

She started moving papers around on the table,

moving closer and closer to Jackson. He continued to focus on whatever captured his attention. He'd pushed up his sleeves and leaned across the table, absorbed by the task in front of him.

Why didn't he realize she needed him?

His eyes flicked to the clock every thirty seconds. Each time, his body stiffened more. His withdrawal meant one thing. This would not end well. He knew Oliver was gone. Perhaps forever. And he couldn't look at her.

A tight lip press sent a bolt of pain streaking up her injured cheek, preventing her mind from pulling on that thread.

She retreated to the basement. She'd fix the bunny. Everything needed to be perfect for when Oliver returned. The cabinet beside the washer and dryer might have her sewing supplies. Her weight landed on each step with more stomp than necessary. Maybe that would get Jackson's attention. She yanked open the cabinet, retrieved her sewing kit, and slammed the door. The lack of a satisfying bang infuriated her as the soft-close hinges Jackson had installed functioned perfectly. She stomped up the staircase.

She pushed her way back into the living room, and her gaze collided with Meg's. Instantly, pressure built behind her eyes until the thought they might pop from her skull.

Meg's lifted eyebrows meant she'd heard Kim's clomping, and still, her friend didn't ask the pointless question everyone seemed to ask. Meg already knew that Kim wasn't okay. She would never be okay again. Meg threw her arms around Kim. "I'm so sorry."

Kim remained stiff-necked and rigid. If she gave way, if she yielded even one bit, she'd shatter into a million pieces.

Kim had met Meg when Meg applied to Life House. The women's shelter that Kim ran in Sycamore Hill provided counsel to battered women and helped them relaunch into a safer life. Kim had been in a counselling session with Meg, who'd run to Sycamore Hill to escape her ex, when she'd learned that Hayden took Oliver that first time. Their relationship had changed in that moment. Meg became the counsellor and Kim was the one in need of godly wisdom. It was the only time Kim blurred that ethical line and developed a friendship with a client.

A surge of gratitude rushed through her. Meg was God's gift to her. Meg, newly married and established in a good life, radiated hope. She was physical evidence of how God worked on behalf of His children. And Kim needed hope like never before.

Meg took the sewing kit from Kim's hands and led Kim to the couch. She placed the kit on the table.

"Jackson was at church when you called." Meg kept one arm looped through Kim's. They sat thigh to thigh on the sofa. "Emma updated Pastor Owen like you asked her to, and Pastor Owen updated the congregation.

They've been praying ever since. I came as soon as I could."

Kim stared at the bunny positioned on her lap to face her. She stroked one velvety ear.

"Emma promised to keep her phone on her. When they find Oliver—" Meg's voice broke.

Kim loved she spoke with confidence. When. Not if. When.

Meg cleared her throat. "When they find him, she said to call her. She'll meet you wherever and whenever and make sure he's okay."

Emma pretty much said the same thing to her when she looked her over. The ridiculousness of being given a medical all-clear by Emma rang hollow. How could her physical body be fine when she was dying inside? Kim leaned into Meg, needing to feel her friend's presence. She swiped the tears that dripped from her chin. "What am I going to do?"

"Take it one moment at a time." Meg repeated the wisdom that Kim had shared with hundreds of women. "You're going to live in this moment and trust God. No good comes from borrowing tomorrow's fear." Meg wrapped an arm around her shoulder and gently rocked her. "You're going to believe that God loves Oliver, and He knows where He is. Oliver is not alone. The Spirit of God is with him."

Kim didn't know how to live in this moment. Not when the moment held such uncertainty. Not when it separated her from Oliver and undermined her confidence in God's care.

Meg's head pressed close to hers. Her friend's voice dropped to a whisper. "You're going to remember that Oliver is strong. Jackson is looking for him. I'm here as long as you need me. God is bigger than the storm."

Kim's gaze wound its way back to Jackson. Her gut tightened at his contorted expression. Hayden would not call. He didn't want money. He wanted to hurt Kim. Jackson remained unconvinced that Hayden had Oliver. But if it wasn't Hayden, if it was a stranger—

Her stomach cramped. She clutched the bunny to her gut and groaned.

Jackson lifted his head, and their gazes collided. Finally. His jaw tightened, and then he refocused on his work.

Her heart shrank. She was losing him, too.

A part of her had hoped she, Oliver, and Jackson might one day make a family that was more than uncle and nephew. She dreamed of marriage, but right now, he avoided her, failing to comfort her. He withdrew when she needed him the most, working professionally and detached. He'd drawn the lines around their relationship, and she saw them clearly. What if this meant his concern flowed from an uncle, not a potential lover? No. She wasn't thinking straight. Her mind was spinning in irrational circles. That was all.

Fear hit like a foot in the gut.

Her cell rang, and she jumped to her feet. She'd set it

on the table, plugged into a power outlet, in case of a call. The vibration of the ring sent it drifting across the table's surface. She bounded into the room.

"It's a video call," Stuart said.

The ringtone sounded a second time. Her heart hammered her ribs as she reached for her phone. Jackson had changed the phone's settings, so they had several rings before the messaging system kicked in.

A third ring.

Her breath bottled in her throat. Her lungs screamed. What if they hung up?

"His video will be on," Jackson said. "Keep the screen centered on your face. Don't let him see us in the background."

She nodded. Her throat swelled. Black spots bounced in her peripheral vision. What if she couldn't speak?

A fourth ring.

What if she missed her chance to save Oliver? She paced in front of the table. What if—

Jackson readied his phone to record her phone screen. "Say what I told you to say."

Meg and Stuart hushed.

Kim pressed the button that allowed her to accept the video call. By the grace of God, the thickness in her throat decreased, and she squeaked out, "Hello?"

The phone screen lit up. Oliver sat at a table, stacking jumbo blocks. A juice box with a straw was open beside him. He was fine.

Kim clutched the phone. "Oliver!"

He didn't react.

Kim swayed, and Meg stepped behind her and supported her elbows.

Meg, not Jackson.

Oliver appeared unhurt. His skin blotchy from crying, clothing intact, no visible wounds.

"You can see he is safe, but he cannot see you or hear you." A mechanical voice filled her dining room. "Tell us where to find El, and Oliver will stay safe."

Kim's gaze zipped to Jackson's. She'd been prepared for Hayden. Maybe even a ransom demand. But not this.

Stuart held up a sheet of paper. *Who is El?*

"Why did you take Oliver?"

Jackson frowned. She flicked her gaze away.

"I don't have time for questions. Where's El?"

"El? I don't know an El."

Stuart held up another sheet of paper. *Short for Ellie? Elena?* Jackson mouthed.

The blood drained from her head. Kim staggered. Meg's increased pressure on her elbows was the only reason Kim remained upright as fogginess crept at the edges of her vision. Kim clawed it back. She fell against Meg. Her head felt too heavy for her neck, ears roaring. All the moisture evaporated in her mouth.

"You remember her. That's good," the voice said. "You have until ten o'clock to give me her location." The caller hung up. Oliver's video feed disappeared.

"No—" Kim's head buzzed. This was about Elena

Watters. She twisted into Meg's arms. Ten o'clock. Forty-five minutes.

"Who is El?" Meg's soft question brushed against her ear. It was as if she knew.

"Elena Watters checked into Life House yesterday," Kim whispered.

Meg's grip on Kim's arm tightened. Meg knew what it meant to run to a place like Life House. Months ago, Meg's ex had tracked her down to Sycamore Hill, and she'd had to face her greatest fear. Now, similar trouble followed Elena.

Jackson had arrested Meg's ex. Would he be able to stop Elena's?

Kim bent at the waist. Her breaths came in gasps. Elena had left a dangerous man. She had tried leaving him once before, and he found her and dragged her back. It took a positive pregnancy test for her to find the courage to leave him a second time. She'd die to protect her baby.

Elena came directly to Life House, thanks to the contact cards Kim had teams of people distributing all over the province. Kim had welcomed her and given her sanctuary, listening to her story and assuring her they would take the steps needed to protect her and her child. Instead of checking El into the residence house, Kim called Jackson, asking who he'd recommend to host Elena. Her gut told her the woman's ex wouldn't let her go easily, but she'd never guessed how far he'd go.

Spots danced in Kim's vision. Her thundering heart beat deep in her ears. This was her fault. She'd checked El in. She'd put her into protective housing. They'd taken Oliver because of her job.

CHAPTER 4

# *9:30 am.*

Jackson had years on the force. He knew what it was to be the official bearing bad news, the one searching for the lost, the one that longed to give innocent victims answers for their grief. But it had never been like this. He'd never been here. There was a reason officers recused themselves when they had a personal connection. It muddied the water.

Kim's entire body shook. She raised a trembling hand, but somewhere, partway up, it stopped and floated as if she'd forgotten what she was trying to do with it. She knew something. A piece of the puzzle had clicked, and the torment shredded her.

Her breath sounds shallowed, and when she straightened fully, her legs gave way. She collapsed against Meg, and her complexion faded to a sickly gray. She pressed her hand into her chest and clutched the fabric of her shirt.

Before he could insist she tell him what cut her legs from under her, Kim lunged toward the kitchen.

A dining room chair clattered to its side as she shoved it out of her way. A dish shattered on the ceramic tile. Kim moaned at a guttural level. She clawed at the laminate counter's edge and leaned over the sink and heaved.

And heaved.

And heaved.

Her body convulsed while she retched.

Meg beat him to Kim's side, but only by a hair. She slipped an arm around Kim's waist, held back Kim's hair, and did all the things Jackson burned to do but couldn't. The last time he let his emotions rule him at work, the bad guy won. He couldn't let that happen again. Not when it was Oliver's life on the line.

Kim gagged. With her head over the sink, she reached for the faucet. Still leaning over the basin, she rinsed the sink and her mouth.

Jackson hated that he couldn't comfort Kim, but this wasn't about his feelings. Jackson might not be Oliver's dad, but he felt like he was. Ever since he moved to Sycamore Hill, he'd filled the role that Hayden abandoned. Not because he had to, but because he wanted to. But right now, Oliver needed a cop, not an uncle or surrogate father.

He glanced at the clock's constantly moving digits. Stuart had reset the timer, so it counted down to the ten o'clock deadline like a bomb to detonation. When the higher-ups arrived, they'd boot him from the case.

Jackson was too close. This was too personal. But until then, he was in. All in until Oliver came home.

Meg murmured soft words to Kim. The words he wanted to murmur. She rubbed small circles into Kim's back, and his palms itched with a need for physical contact. Meg promised Kim that she would get through this. Meg said Kim was strong.

The back of his throat ached. Meg was right. Kim was the strongest woman Jackson had ever met. She'd been through this before. Not exactly this, but close. When Hayden's parental abduction stretched over a year, Kim never stopped looking for her son. She never lost hope. And when Jackson reunited them, she did the hardest thing for a parent who'd lost her child. She shared him with Jackson and his parents, opening her heart to the family that had unwittingly contributed to her pain. Because that was what Oliver needed. She always put others first.

*Lord, hour by hour, help her—help us—to walk in the strength of the Lord Jesus Christ, trusting Him for all we need and believing His Spirit is with us, strengthening us and upholding us, and comforting us.*

Kim was strong, but God was stronger.

"Tell me more about El." Stuart broke the silence.

Kim stared into the sink. She didn't lift her head, or turn toward Stuart's voice, or acknowledge his question.

"Is El who you took to the farm?" Jackson's brief time in Sycamore Hill was long enough to meet the guys that'd have his back. A small police presence often called on the community in the initial crisis moments, and he made it his pattern to seek men of honor and cultivate relationships with them in every place he served. Moving here had been no different. So, when Kim called about a new client in need of a safe place, Jackson suggested Willow Creek Farms.

"Yes." She continued to stare into the sink.

*Come on, baby, stay with me. Tell me what I need to know.* Then she could fall apart because he'd carry it from there. "Is El still at the farm?"

Vacant eyes lifted to his. He saw how his tone hurt her, but he didn't have time to coddle her feelings. Not when that blasted clock lost a precious minute every sixty seconds.

Kim nodded.

Jackson locked gazes with Stuart. "She's at Willow Creek Farms. I gotta call Simon."

Matt Gaither, a local army man, had introduced Jackson to Simon and Colleen Willow. Simon had served his country before retiring, and Colleen was no slouch. Used to running the farm alone when her husband was on leave, she'd fought off wild animals trying to feast on her chickens and even scared the occasional intruder away. They knew how to defend the defenseless.

Simon answered before the first ring completed, and Jackson updated him on the potential trouble coming his way.

Meg helped Kim to a chair at the kitchen table. She

poured her another coffee. Both women avoided meeting his eyes.

"Stuart, do we have someone you can send to Life House?"

"Already on it." Stuart didn't look up from his phone. His thumbs pounded the keys in a text message. "I redirected Noah. If we're lucky, whoever has Oliver first searched Life House offices looking for Elena and left us some clues."

Lord willing, they'd have something to work with soon.

Jackson's gaze drilled into Kim's profile. She hadn't looked his way since his harsh questioning. She didn't understand he needed to shock her back to the present moment. Her urge to retreat was strong, but she needed to fight it and tell him what he needed to know. How much did God expect one woman to carry? Kim's experience with Hayden made her more sensitive to the trauma the women brought with them to Life House. Jackson loved her strength, but even the strongest person broke under the right pressure.

*Lord, if it's possible, let this cup of suffering pass.*

Jesus prayed that prayer, and God said no. Jesus took the ultimate cup for them. A famous pastor once said that Jesus bought endurance for His children through the cup poured out, the new covenant in His blood. And they needed endurance. Kim. Him. Oliver. They needed a strength they didn't have in themselves.

"Let's review the facts," Stuart said. "Whoever has

Oliver wants to trade him for Elena Watters. Tell me about Elena."

Kim's glassy eyes stared past them.

"Kim," Jackson prompted. Her blinkless gaze tripped his heart. "Look at me." Jackson's need for sharpness shredded his soul.

Kim finally turned her face. She looked him dead in the eyes, and he nearly staggered. Her nostrils flared. Sweat beaded on her forehead. Her upper lip curled, exposing a slice of teeth.

He could work with angry. If she needed to hate him, so be it. He'd do whatever he had to, even though it churned his gut. "Tell Stuart about Elena."

Kim was spiraling fast, and Jackson needed her engaged and alert. Oliver needed her to be strong, stronger than she'd ever had to be. But he believed in her. God was with her. And that was what a mother did. They dug deep.

He ignored the judgement oozing from Meg. He didn't have time to explain the need for his methods. Not if the guy holding Oliver was Elena's ex-boyfriend. Jackson hadn't gone with Kim and Elena last night, but he documented his role in suggesting the farm and looked into Elena's ex, because if trouble was headed for Sycamore Hill, he wanted to be ready.

Kim licked her lips. Her eyes dulled to an acceptance that made his insides shrivel. "She was afraid her ex would follow her. He's obsessed with his baby."

Stuart nodded. "What else?"

Kim disconnected further. "He's dangerous. Connected with a gang in the city."

Reality slammed Jackson against the ropes. He and Kim might not recover from this fight. He'd seen it in other couples, in other cases. Tragedy and the tensions involved in kidnappings had ripped relationships more solid than theirs to shreds. But Oliver mattered more. Bringing Oliver home mattered more than comforting the woman he loved, grieving with her, praying with her, crying with her, no matter how much he wanted to pull her into his arms and promise her that everything was going to be okay. The reality hit him so hard it hurt to breathe. Indulging those emotions wasn't an option.

Jackson would comfort Kim tomorrow. He would fall apart and grieve for Oliver tomorrow. Tomorrow, he'd be everything Kim needed him to be. Today, he had to stuff his emotions to bring Oliver back, because anything less was unacceptable. Unthinkable. Not survivable.

Jackson forced his aching arms to stay at his side. Meg would hold Kim after he left. Meg would comfort her because Meg wasn't able to do the one thing Jackson could—bring Oliver home. He prayed Kim would understand why it had to be this way. "I think it's time I had a chat with Elena."

"You can't work the case."

Stuart's abrupt reminder made his steps hitch. Stuart was right. But not working on the case wasn't going to happen.

"I'll call our Staff again." Stuart picked up his cell. "We might need more than the Missing Persons unit. We might need Guns and Gangs."

El's ex was a notorious criminal with a long rap sheet. It complicated things. Oliver's chances of return grew slimmer by the second. The case snowballing downhill morphed into an avalanche that threatened to bury them. "I'll speak with Elena."

"Jackson—" Stuart pounded a fist on the table, jolting him. "You can't work the case."

"I can put information together for the Missing Persons unit."

Stuart held his gaze for a minute before giving a curt nod. "But that's it."

Jackson touched Kim's arm, and her head jerked. "I need to speak with Elena."

"She might not talk to you."

"Elena doesn't have a choice." Jackson notified Simon via text that he was on his way.

Thank the Lord for Meg. Meg's soft tone soothed Kim's bruises. Kim needed her community to be strong for her. God would work through His people.

Tension dialled up and pressure increased behind his eyes. He loved Kim and Oliver so much that it physically hurt. He bit his cheek until he tasted blood.

Stuart's hand landed heavily on Jackson's shoulder. "I just got off the phone with the Missing Persons detective assigned to the case."

"Who is it?"

"Burland."

Jackson nodded. Burland was good. They'd met at a conference once. Burland would maintain communication with Stuart and their Staff Sergeant as he and his team travelled, so everyone stayed updated.

"Guns and gangs will be here ASAP. But the weather and highway conditions mean we might be it for the next few hours."

The gang unit was just as far away as the kidnapping unit.

Jackson nodded. "We're gonna get this guy. We'll find Oliver and bring him home. This ends today."

Stuart ignored Jackson's use of the word we.

Kim's eyes shone, and Meg lifted her chin a notch. Jackson had finally done something right. He was going to rain hell on the man who'd hurt his family.

# CHAPTER 5

# 9:45 a.m.

K im pulled away from Meg. If Jackson was going to see Elena, so was she. "I'm coming with you."

He flattened his lips. "You're not. You can't."

"Your supervisor said I wasn't to be alone." She raised her chin, pushing her tongue against the back of her teeth as she weighed her options.

"You're not alone."

Swallowing the last trace of bitter bile, Kim shrugged, not needing his permission. "I can't find Oliver myself. I'm not able to stop this from unfolding, but I can, with absolute certainty, drive to where Elena is located." She levelled a look at him she reserved for Oliver's worst tantrums. He was not sidelining her. Not now. Not when it came to Oliver. She practically dared him to stop her.

From the corner of her eye, she caught Stuart

sneaking glances their way, curious who would emerge the victor in this battle of wills.

The stiff lines on Jackson's face relaxed. He smiled like an adult indulging a child, or a superior tolerating a subordinate. It riled her so much she could have churned butter out of her ears.

"Your car is in the ditch on Holiday Drive. How do you plan to get there?"

Kim extended her palm toward Meg and without missing a beat said, "I'll take Meg's car."

Meg dashed for her purse and retrieved her keys. She plopped them into Kim's hand and raised her chin. It only wobbled a bit. "She'll use mine."

Meg's declaration lacked assurance. Her voice lifted on the last word like her statement was a question. Kim got it. She wasn't as confident as she pretended to be, either. Nothing about what went down today made her feel hopeful. But all that mattered was that she was going. There wasn't anything he could do about it.

"I could detain you for interfering with an investigation."

Except that. He could do that. Her empty stomach turned over. She pressed a hand against it and closed her eyes. "But you won't." At least she hoped he wouldn't. "We both know it." Kim stuffed her arms into her winter coat, grabbed her purse, and stomped to the front door. Every eye in the room followed her.

She lifted her chin. "I'm leaving. If you're heading in

the same direction, I'd prefer to ride with you. But I'm going. End of discussion."

This was her olive branch. If Jackson didn't take it, they'd never recover. She needed to be part of the solution. And he needed to let her. If he kept shutting her out, if she stayed on the sidelines and something happened . . . She swallowed again. A mouthful of air bubbled in her gut.

"I'll stay with her," Stuart said. "You go. We'll be fine."

Kim swung her gaze to Stuart. "But—"

"No buts." Stuart's glare left no wiggle room. "You will not go. And the longer we argue, the less time we have to find Oliver." He flicked his gaze to Jackson and tossed his keys to him. "I've got this covered. Take the cruiser."

Jackson caught the keys one-handed. The front door closed behind him. Kim fisted her hands at her side. She lifted her face, ready to rip into Stuart, but stopped short, thrown by the brokenness and compassion in his gaze.

"There isn't much Jackson can do. He's too close to this. Let him go. He loves Oliver, too."

Her mouth trembled.

"Soon, the Missing Persons detective will take over. The information Jackson is gathering can help the team, but he can't do it if you're with him."

She chewed her bottom lip. Her mind understood why it had to be this way, but her heart didn't. If she opened her mouth even the tiniest bit, she'd cry. And if she started crying, she would never stop.

Kim nodded. Her dry tongue bumped over her lips. She cleared her throat. "Can I use my phone? I want to see my notes on Elena."

A smile softened the hard lines of Stuart's face. He disconnected the phone from the power supply and handed it to Kim. "That's a good idea."

As Stuart returned his attention to his computer screen, Kim nudged Meg with her foot. "Distract him." She tipped her head in his direction. "I'm going after Jackson."

Meg's eyes widened.

"Give me a five-minute head start."

Meg mouthed, *no*, but Kim ignored her.

Kim slipped into her bedroom, grabbed an old jacket, and tiptoed to the back door. She winced as it creaked open. Once outside, she hurried to Meg's vehicle. In less than a minute, she was headed toward the farm. Elena owed her some answers.

She approached the last intersection before leaving the town limits, thankful the snow had stopped. The wind played with the accumulation like a cat tossing its prey, but at least it wouldn't get any deeper. The stoplight turned red, and her gaze connected with the driver in front of her via his rearview mirror. *Uh oh.*

The cruiser's lights swirled on and it pulled to the side of the road. Kim followed and lowered her window.

Jackson stormed toward her. His nostrils flared and

white huffs of exhalations shot from them like steam. "Are you trying to get Oliver killed?"

Her head fuzzed. All she heard were the words *Oliver*, and *killed*.

"You can't be here. It goes against protocol."

Energy surged through her. "I don't care about protocol!"

Jackson pounded the vehicle's roof. "You have to go back."

"I can't be alone."

He shoved off the car, twisting away. His fingers dug into his hair.

"Jackson—" It came out all broken and distraught. He had to understand. She couldn't stay still as someone used Oliver to manipulate her. Not a second time.

"Promise to do exactly what I say." With his defenses lowered, she glimpsed his turmoil. He pressed both hands against the frame of the vehicle and leaned in, his vulnerability nearly undoing her. "I can't lose you, too."

Five gruff words gave her a peek at the heart beating behind the badge. He was still there. Somewhere under the shield was the man she loved, and it filled her with hope.

"Park in the bank's empty lot and get in with me."

She nodded and raised the window as he returned to the cruiser. She followed his instructions and locked Meg's vehicle. The rawness of their interaction reached places in her heart that she hadn't visited in a long time, and she melted a little. Not enough to follow protocol, but sufficient to climb into his passenger seat and lean across the console to press her palm against his unshaven cheek. She tipped her forehead against his. The bristles on his jawline scraped her soft skin, contrasting their God-ordained differences. It made her feel secure. Jackson would keep her safe.

"You won't lose me. You can't."

They lingered for less than a second before controlled detachment dropped back over Jackson's face. But this time, she saw it for what it was. Self-protection. Jackson was afraid.

And that terrified her on a whole new level.

Kim buckled her seatbelt and didn't say a word. She stared straight ahead, praying over and over the only words she could think. *Please, Jesus.*

He backed out of his parking spot and wound their way to the farm.

*Please, Jesus.*

Silence cranked the tension in the cab, broken only when Jackson announced, "We have a tail."

Kim rotated to look over her shoulder. "Who follows a cop?"

The muscle at the hinge of his jawline twitched. "Someone who just told you the price of Oliver's return."

They couldn't find El. Her plan worked. Her gut had been right to stash the woman somewhere safer than the Life House residence.

The SUV followed their turn. And the next.

Kim squinted, but her view was obscured. She'd

promised El that her ex wouldn't locate her. But that was before he took Oliver. Before she understood the personal cost. "They wouldn't be stupid enough to grab El in front of a cop, would they?"

"No, but they'll make a plan to snatch her later while we are making a transfer. A person is most vulnerable then." Jackson stabbed the speaker on his phone and hit redial. The call connected to the vehicle's Bluetooth.

Jackson's world baffled Kim. He lived with dim statistics and constant heartbreak. Yet, he never hardened. He remained the kindest, noblest, most gentle man she'd ever known. They'd been practically co-parenting Oliver for over a year. She couldn't imagine a future without him. But he'd never kissed her beyond a chaste peck on the cheek or forehead. He never pushed for more than she was ready to give. Yet their connection seemed more intimate than friendship. Deeper. Rooted in the rich soil of shared faith and their love for a little boy.

The phone call connected. Kim recognized Simon's voice.

Jackson changed lanes and took a fast right. The back end fishtailed, but Jackson steered out of it. The cruisers were always winter ready, which was more than she could say for the vehicle following them. It hit the brakes too hard and arced. Each swing was bigger until they missed the turn.

Her breath shot out.

"Simon, I'm on my way to you. Elena's ex is trying to

smoke her out. Stash her in the safe spot we talked about."

Kim snapped her eyes to Jackson. A new hideaway was news to her.

All the usual joviality in Simon's tone evaporated. He'd reverted to his army persona. "Yes, sir."

"Be there in ten. I need to make sure we lost the tail." Jackson disconnected. He glanced at her, his attention dropping to her white knuckles clutching the seatbelt.

"I've seen enough ditches today." She loosened her fingers.

"You should have stayed home." The muscle in his jaw twitched with the regularity of a pulse. "We could protect you there."

"When Oliver's in a safe place, I'll stay with him. Until then, you're stuck with me."

He chewed on his lip. A sharp whistle emitted from his nose. After a long, uncomfortable pause, he spoke. "I'm gonna drive a few more minutes. When I know it's clear, we'll double back in the right direction."

They rode in silence, each lost in their thoughts and fears until she broke the stillness. "What's the plan?"

She knew there wasn't a bone in Jackson's body that would sacrifice one vulnerable person for another. That meant he had an idea that was better than the horrible one simmering inside of her. Refining fires brought dross to the surface, and as the flames increased, the scum in her heart rose. Yesterday, she wouldn't have thought she'd ever consider betraying a client. Today, she not only considered it; she almost hoped it could be that easy to bring Oliver home.

And she hated herself for it.

"We aren't trading Elena. But we won't let Oliver die, either."

Pressure built behind her eyes. He hadn't really answered her question. Was it because the plan was confidential or because he didn't have one?

*Please, Jesus.*

She turned to the window, and the trees sped past. Oliver was nearby. But where? Was he crying? Hurt? Did he understand the danger?

She yanked her cuff over her fist and wiped her eyes.

*Please, Jesus.*

Jackson pulled into the laneway of Willow Creek farms. Simon was waiting on the porch. He bounded down the steps and met them at the car.

Kim fumbled with the door handle. Why wasn't he with Elena? Did something happen?

"El is gone," Simon blurted.

Kim's hurried movements froze.

"What do you mean, gone?" Jackson slammed the cruiser's door.

The men swirled in front of her. Kim's new goal became exiting the car. Remaining upright. Staying conscious. It took all her energy and focus. She opened the door.

Right behind those basic goals screamed the questions that never stopped. Did they take El? Did her ex beat them there? Was the tail a misdirect?

She climbed out of the cruiser. If Elena had fallen prey to the violent man, at least they wouldn't hurt her. Not until the baby was born. Light-headedness made her stumble. Her hands went numb as she twisted them. She moved toward Jackson, legs like tree trunks, propelled by a force impossible to resist. If they had Elena, what did that mean for Oliver?

Simon was speaking. His lips were moving. But Kim couldn't hear anything over the screaming inside her head.

# CHAPTER 6

# 9:57 a.m.

J ackson's heart rattled against his ribs like a jailed man desperate to break free. 9:57. The kidnappers were calling in three minutes, and Elena was gone. He had no intention of handing her over, but he'd been counting on the woman's insight to navigate conversing with Oliver's abductors.

Simon's succinct update left little hope.

"She could still be here, right? On the farm?" Kim's gaze darted around the property. The hopefulness in her voice scrambled for a hold as her hands flapped in front of her body. She looked his way, but focused on something beyond him. Like it took all her strength and mental energy to remain engaged. She was grasping.

Jackson got it. It was all too fluid. Unstable.

9:58. Two minutes.

"I doubt it." Jackson squeezed the sides of his head. He

paced a few steps away. Elena was hiding from a dangerous man, so she wouldn't stroll around a strange property. If she wasn't in her room, she was gone. His hands dropped to massage the tight knot in his neck. This threw in a wrench their engine didn't need. "Did she leave of her own volition?"

Less than two minutes. The clock never stopped ticking. One hundred and twenty seconds. It wasn't enough time. It howled in his ears.

Kim cradled her cell phone in her hands.

Watching.

Waiting.

"No signs of a struggle. I've searched the house and was going to start on the property when you pulled up. Brown's out searching the back woods. Elena's footprints led through the orchard."

"Noah?" Stuart had sent him to Life House.

"Constable James called when he realized Kim was gone." Simon's gaze flicked to Kim, who blushed. "He said Brown would approach from the south side. He's working his way across the property. I expect he'll reach the house in less than fifteen minutes."

Kim hugged herself as her head swivelled between Simon and Jackson. The snow crunched under her shifting weight. "What are we going to do?"

Jackson's skin prickled. She expected him to know. Stuart had pulled Noah. That was a good call. "We'll look at Elena's room. You'll stay with Colleen."

For once, she didn't argue.

But first, they had another phone call. Any minute now. Less than sixty seconds.

Simon's feet spread shoulder width apart. His arms hung loose at the sides, but the tension radiating from him belied his casual posture. Army men never changed. Like Kim, Simon looked to Jackson for direction, but he still didn't have any to offer.

"Elena rabbited." Simon said. "I don't know what spooked her. When Colleen left her in her room, Elena said she was exhausted, so we gave her some space. I monitored the doors. She didn't leave through either of them."

They'd lost a woman. A pregnant woman. A woman who probably climbed out the bedroom window and hoofed it on foot without a jacket or winter clothing. If she didn't find warm shelter, her biggest concern wouldn't be the man chasing her. It would be the harsh elements.

Jackson bit back a roar. The cold burned his lungs. The alternative theory was that the kidnappers had found her. And if they had Elena, would they even call? Was Oliver already—

Don't go there.

9:59.

Kim's gaze ping-ponged between him and Simon. "What does this mean for Oliver?"

Simon was one of the good guys. There was no way someone hoodwinked him. Elena left of her own free will. But why?

"It means things just got harder." Jackson spoke through his teeth. A lot harder. He pinched his forehead, trying to force his thoughts to slow. "When they call, don't let on that Elena is gone."

"But if they have her, they'll know I'm lying."

"And if they don't have her, it'll buy Oliver time."

The phone rang. Jackson locked eyes with Kim. He placed both his hands over hers, covering the phone and muffling it. "You can do this. Blame me. Say the police moved her, and that you're trying to figure out where. If they say they've got her, play dumb."

Simon had his cell ready and started recording.

She was white-faced and desperate. Kim needed him to be strong, sure about their plan, not guessing at the last minute.

A noise gurgled in her throat.

"You can do this." He let go of her.

She tapped the phone's speaker option and moved it closer to Simon's device. "Hello?"

"Are you ready to give her up?"

Jackson's heart thumped. *Thank you, Lord!* They didn't have Elena. They didn't know she was missing.

A look almost akin to joy crossed Kim's face. *Hope.* Jackson's heart lurched. Hope was dangerous. Hope increased the devastation of a negative outcome. He leaned forward. *Come on, Kim. Sell it. You can do it.*

Kim jutted her chin. "The police moved her in the night. I don't know where."

The mechanical voice swore. "I said no cops!"

"No, you didn't!" Her outburst shocked everyone, including the caller.

Silence.

"But I'll find her." Kim squeezed the phone until Jackson thought it might break. "I just need a bit of time." Sobs now intermixed with her words. "Please don't hurt Oliver. Please don't hurt him."

Kim heaved. Jackson could barely understand her words. It was all too much. She was losing it.

"You have one hour, or your boy dies." The call disconnected.

Kim fell into Jackson's arms. She shook and buried her face in his shoulder, and it muffled her cries. Better people had broken under less. She'd handled it like a pro.

"I can't do this. I can't. I can't. I can't."

"You did good." Jackson rocked her. "You bought us an hour. It was good."

Jackson looked over her head at Simon. He needed Simon. The kidnapping unit was still too far out. Guns and gangs even further. Other OPP officers from nearby towns should roll in soon, but they weren't here yet.

Simon nodded, fully understanding the unspoken question. "We are getting her boy back."

Jackson's chest swelled. Hope was dangerous.

He tightened his arms around Kim and pressed his mouth to her hair. "Yes, we are."

Oliver was gone over a year when Hayden took him. Jackson would not let Kim lose Oliver a second time. Not even if it killed him.

. . .

Inside the farmhouse, Jackson kept Kim in his peripheral vision. Colleen placed a steaming mug in front of her. Kim wrapped her hands around it and pulled it forward. The steam drifted over her face. She never lifted the mug to her lips. She closed her puffy and red-rimmed eyes.

Colleen retreated to the kitchen, where she kept adding to a mountain of sandwiches. The men had to eat, she'd said, stuffing one into Jackson's hand.

It was a little past ten in the morning. The idea of food made his stomach roll, but Colleen was right. It could be hours before he'd get another chance to refuel. If he didn't eat, he might not have the strength he needed. He bit into the sandwich and chewed. Colleen made a good hoagie, but today it ground up like sawdust in his mouth. He forced himself to ingest the nutrition for Oliver.

Kim's meal sat untouched in front of her.

Jackson had called his Staff Sergeant and updated him on Elena's disappearance. The man wasn't happy that Kim tricked PC James and was now with Jackson, but there wasn't much he could do about it now. Jackson couldn't send her back to the house alone, especially when they considered the tail they had coming here.

Jackson emailed the phone call recording to his Staff. His Staff would update Detective Burland, who was still en route. Considering what they knew about Elena and her ex, she had to be the key. If they figured out her history, they'd figure out who she trusted and where she went.

Simon cleared his throat, and Jackson looked up.

Simon stood in the doorway, leaning a shoulder against the wall. He tipped his head toward the hallway, and Jackson pushed back from the table to join him.

"What do we know so far?" Simon kept his voice low so the women wouldn't be able to hear them.

Jackson darted a glance to Kim. She sat at the far end of the table with her feet hooked around the chair legs. Her vacant expression made him suspect she'd retreated to someplace safe in her mind.

Simon deserved more details than he got last night. The people who helped the residents of Life House walked a fine line of respecting the client's privacy and getting enough details to help them. When Kim dropped Elena off, she asked Simon to "keep watch." It was code for "trouble might come knocking."

On those nights, the man slept in a rocker by the window. From that position, he had a line of sight to his front and back doors, the laneway, and half the property. And he did it all covertly. The women were clueless about the sleep Simon lost for them. And Simon never asked for more information. But today, Simon's request for details was a fair one. They'd dumped a truckload of trouble on his land. He had a right to know what kind of missile was locked on its target.

Jackson leaned back in his chair. "Elena's dating a well-known gang leader in the city."

"Who's the leader?"

"Nathan Fieldstone."

"Why the fixation on Watters?"

"Nathan had a child with a former girlfriend. The child died in the crossfire of a gunfight with a rival gang. Then Nathan shot the mother for not protecting his kid. He's obsessed with ensuring this child lives to inherit his empire."

"El will never be free of him. A child binds you for life."

The men spun. How long had Kim been standing there listening? Judging from her expression, too long. Her eyes were heavy and her face pinched.

Jackson's gut clenched. Was that how she felt about Hayden? Bound forever? The truth hit below the belt. If Kim ever considered marriage, it should be to the father of her child, especially if Hayden had really changed, like he claimed. Jackson had been praying for years that his brother would repent. Could God be answering his prayers now? Would He do it like this? Was this God's way of reminding Jackson that he had no business hoping he'd ever be more than Oliver's uncle? But it might not matter. If he failed to bring Oliver home, Kim would blame him forever.

"Guys like Nathan don't stop coming." Simon folded his arms across his broad chest. "He wants his kid. She probably figured they'd track her here. But how? Why was she so certain they'd find where we hid her?"

"When the baby's born, he'll have no need for her,"

Kim said. "She knows what happened to the last woman."

"We have an hour." Jackson strode back into the dining room. "An hour to find her, and an hour to save Oliver."

Simon followed him. "What's Missing Persons' ETA?"

"They're en route. The soonest they'll get here is eleven o'clock this morning." Jackson looked out the window. The storm had cleared. Still, copious amounts of snow blocked many of the roads. "Unless the plows are out, it's going to be longer."

"This is on us." Simon's head bobbed, accepting the reality.

"It's on us," Jackson echoed.

Jackson trusted Simon to have his back. Noah would emerge from his search through the woods any minute, and they would make a plan together. These guys had battled evil before. They didn't scare easy, and they wouldn't back down. There wasn't a better team. But a bigger one would be nice.

# CHAPTER 7

# 10:30 a.m.

"El's phone." The sentence fragment popped out as Kim's brain moved faster than her mouth. Intake at Life House involved safety precautions. One thing Kim drilled into the women was to ditch their cell if they felt like they were in immediate danger. Many apps made locating a victim easy for a predator.

Simon frowned. "We never found it. I assumed she took it with her."

"If Elena brought her phone here, she would have known they could track her through it. She'd toss it if something spooked her." Fresh energy infused Kim. The device could hold information as to where she could have gone. "It's got to be close by."

Colleen entered from the kitchen and rubbed Simon's shoulders. "We searched the house."

"She might have held onto it for a while." Regardless of how deep Kim drilled that hole, the women she counselled refused to give up their devices until it became necessary. Elena would be no different.

Colleen gestured down the hall. "I can take you to her room."

Colleen led Kim down the corridor, and Jackson followed them. He didn't walk beside her, hold her hand, or offer any kind of comfort to her. He'd retreated again, and his physical and emotional withdrawal continued to sting. Jackson was doing everything he could to find Oliver. She believed it with her whole heart. Still, something between them had shifted. What if it never shifted back?

Her middle tightened, and the need to purge whatever remained in her stomach welled up in her throat. Kim wanted to rewind the morning. Oliver would spill his cereal at breakfast, and this time, she'd laugh. She'd tell him not to hurry while searching for his bunny. He'd zip his own jacket, and they'd be late for church. Kim fisted a hand against her mouth. She gulped a sob.

Colleen wrapped an arm around her shoulder and pulled her against her side. Colleen. Not Jackson. Kim teetered on the edge of losing the two people she loved the most.

They stopped at the last door. Colleen motioned for Kim to enter. The bedroom was a simple design. A single bed with a round bedside table, a desk, dresser, and closet. Kim recognized the duffle bag open on the foot of the mattress as one of the emergency go bags from Life House. Volunteers packed them with donated clothes and toiletries for cases like Elena's. There would be nothing personal in there. Still, Jackson rooted through it.

The window opened to the orchard, and all Kim could see were rows of dormant peach trees waving their snow-covered branches. Bush stretched behind the peach trees. The wind screamed around the corner of the house, verbalizing the howl Kim held back. Standing in the middle of the room, she rubbed her hands up and down her arms, and friction sent a shiver up her spine. Closing her eyes, she put herself into Elena's mind. She didn't need to know her well to get a feel for her character. Filling out the shelter's intake forms revealed a lot. The questions provided her with a bit of insight. Kim's lungs expanded. If she were Elena and trying to hide her phone to buy herself some time, she'd do her best to not implicate the family that sheltered her. Kim's eyes snapped open. "It won't be in the room."

"How do you know?" Jackson opened and closed empty dresser drawers. Elena hadn't even unpacked.

"She wouldn't lure the danger into Colleen's home."

Jackson's frown rubbed her frayed edges.

"She just wouldn't."

"Simon didn't see Elena leave, and he was by the front door. Nothing suggests she used the back one. That leaves the window." Jackson stood in front of the room's only window. He folded his arms across his chest.

"If Elena tossed the phone out there, it'd be buried by now." Kim rapped her knuckles against her forehead.

*Come on, Lord. A little help!* Elena heard Kim's suggested precautions, so outside was the most logical place. But panicked people got confused. And the possibility remained that Elena's disappearance had nothing to do with being spooked by her ex's henchmen. She might have changed her mind. Elena wouldn't be the first battered woman to return to her abuser.

But she didn't strike Kim as the type to go back. She'd worked too hard to escape. And when a child entered the picture, women found reserves of strength. She'd seen it repeatedly. Elena didn't go back. But something made her feel unsafe.

The phone was their best shot.

"I'll call James and ask him to call the phone company's Corporate Securities department. They can provide the last known tower the phone pinged off." Jackson slipped into the hallway.

Kim opened the window. A rush of cold air cooled her hot skin.

Colleen peered over Kim's shoulder. "That's strange. These windows should have screens."

This was Elena's exit. Kim was sure of it.

Gripping the sill, Kim leaned outside. A rectangular outline was faintly visible. She'd bet her month's wages the window screen was buried underneath. A pattern of slight depressions in the snow led from the window. *Footprints!* They were nearly filled in, but the imprints were there. Kim hoisted herself onto the ledge and swung her feet over the sill.

"What are you doing?" Colleen fumbled for Kim's arm. She threw a frantic look in the direction Jackson had gone, but he'd wandered away.

"I'm finding that phone before the wind buries it until spring." The bedroom was on the first level. The drop wasn't far.

"Wait for Jackson."

Kim shook off Colleen's grip and dropped. The crusty top layer of snow crunched as she landed. There wasn't time to wait. Once the kidnappers figured out Elena was gone, they wouldn't need Oliver. Especially if Oliver saw their faces. Kim's stomach cramped. Elena's ex didn't seem to be the type of guy to leave witnesses, no matter how little or unreliable they might be.

"Jackson!" Colleen shouted.

Kim's cheeks numbed as the wind burned them. Leaving her jacket was a calculated choice that enabled her to avoid questions they didn't have time for. Drifting snow was filling in the footprints. Soon the trail would disappear.

"Wait for Jackson." Colleen shouted out the window.

Kim crouched, trying to get low enough to view the snow's surface at eye level. The subtle, sunken walking pattern led to the peach trees. Her heart quickened. Her breadcrumb path blew over and disappeared right before her eyes.

"I got a trail. I'm gonna see where it leads." Kim

called up to Colleen as she pointed toward the trees. "Tell Jackson he can follow my tracks and catch up."

The further Kim got from the house, the louder the quiet sounded. There was a crispness in the wind. It had an edge and screamed winter wasn't finished with them yet. Ice cracked behind her.

*Jackson.*

Kim spun, a greeting on her lips, but only saw trees and white. The wind's whistle threatened to deafen her calls if she ran into trouble. Yeah, she should have waited for Jackson. Would'a, could'a, should'a, but didn't.

She hugged herself, unable to ward off the chill. How long until frostbite became a concern?

More footfalls.

Her ears strained. Animal or human? Her palms dampened. She retracted them into her sleeves. A rapidly swelling throat choked off any hope of calling for help.

What animals lived in the area? Which ones hibernated and which ones were cold and hungry? Should she call out? What if it was Nathan? Or one of his men? She should have waited.

A hand landed on her shoulder at the same time someone said her name.

Kim yelped and spun. She raked her nails down a body, but only pressed them into a winter jacket. Her vision tunneled. A badge.

"Ma'am, I'm Officer Noah Brown."

The cloudiness in her eyes cleared.

More heavy steps. Thrashing. Constable Brown

shoved her behind him as Jackson burst through the trees with his gun drawn. His wildness softened when he recognized his co-worker. Chest heaving, he holstered his weapon, and Kim noted the intensity in his face.

"We don't have time to waste like this."

The correction stung.

"Let it go." Noah shrugged out of his jacket and threw it over Kim's shivering body. He squeezed her shoulders, the pressure grounding her. "You both love Oliver. Turning on each other won't help."

He was right. "I'm sorry. I was worried about losing the trail."

"In happier news, look what I found." Noah wiggled a phone.

"You got it!" Energy surged through Kim. "I knew it had to be out here."

"The cold has drained the battery. I was heading to the house for a charger when I saw you."

None of that mattered. They had El's phone. There'd be a lead on it. There had to be.

They hurried to the house. Jackson never spoke a word, but he didn't need to. His stony expression and stiff movements said enough. Even after warming up with two cups of coffee, something separated them.

"It's ready," Jackson said.

Kim joined the others crowding around the device, and Jackson powered it on. The home screen lit up. When face recognition didn't work, it reverted to its lock screen, which showed clips of the most recent messages.

"Who's Quinn?" Simon's forehead wrinkled.

Someone named Quinn had asked El for help. That was all they'd get until they unlocked the cell.

"Elena never mentioned a Quinn." Kim's shoulder brushed against Jackson's, and he stepped away.

"Quinn could be a short form, a nickname, code."

Making it even harder to find the person.

"How much of Elena's past did you cover during the intake?" Jackson still didn't look at her. Not really. Not the way she wanted him to.

"Our initial meeting wasn't going over history as much as it was implementing an emergency care plan. Gathering information comes later. After the crisis has passed."

Jackson massaged his jaw. "This could be Nathan trying to lure Elena out."

Kim wove her fingers from both hands into her hair and rubbed her scalp. If the phone didn't help, they had nothing. "I'll go through my file, but I'm sure I'd remember Quinn. It's an unusual enough name."

"Elena never mentioned Quinn to me, either." Colleen's forehead creased. "And I was asking questions about her friends and hometown."

"Stuart radioed to say the Missing Persons unit's ETA is fifteen minutes. Kim and I can take the phone to the house. The IT guy should be able to unlock it."

Jackson was already stuffing his arms into his coat. "And I want to search around here."

"Take Simon," Noah said. "I told him where to go."

Jackson's hurried movements paused. He and Constable Brown exchanged a look that made Kim's heart gallop.

"What aren't you telling me?"

Jackson diverted. "We only have thirty minutes before they call again. It's time to divide and conquer. Noah, can you take Kim to Life House so she can get her files on Elena and then get the phone to the Missing Persons unit? I'll stay here with Simon and follow up on Noah's lead."

Kim's head swivelled between them. They held something back. She felt it in her gut.

# CHAPTER 8

# *10:40 a.m.*

"What did Noah find?" As soon as Kim was out of earshot, Jackson zeroed in on Simon. Noah wouldn't have suggested they separate unless he found something he didn't want Kim to see. Something that would upset her. Jackson braced himself.

"It's outside."

Grabbing their winter coats, they set off on foot, trekking deeper into the orchard than before. Jackson's fingers started tingling in under a minute. His ears burned. They didn't have enough protection from the elements. They had a bit of time before frostbite became a risk. Enough to see what concerned Noah. Then regroup and make a plan.

They hiked for several minutes. The soundtrack of their booted feet breaking through the top layer of ice and crunching to the bottom played in a steady rhythm. Jackson kept one eye on the back of his friend and the other on the disappearing animal tracks. They were more likely to encounter deer than something dangerous, but anything was possible.

Someone had travelled the path before them. The slender boot prints mixed with a few sets of wider and longer ones. Jackson snapped a few pictures on his phone. Were they Kim's? Elena's? These tracks went deeper, so they were fresh. Had Elena met someone? Who did she trust enough to share her location with? There were still more questions than answers.

His foggy exhalation puffed in a white vapor. Every step took them further away from the house. The kidnappers would call soon. Noah wouldn't send them on a meaningless hike, which meant this led somewhere. Somewhere important.

Deep breath in. Deep breath out.

They followed the broken twigs and trampled trail. The nearest branches lacked snow and the slick ground slowed them down. Twenty minutes until they called again.

"We're almost there." Simon pointed ahead.

If Jackson squinted, he could just make out a road cutting through the greenery. The wind raced across the small clearing. It molded the snow into sleek curves and peaks. The private road that Simon used for driving large equipment led here, to the end of the field. It dead-ended, so there was no reason for anyone else to take it. Yet the closer they got to the clearing, the more evident the importance of Noah's discovery became. Tire tracks compressed the snow. Several sets. Then he saw the dark patches.

*No, no, no, no, no.*

Jackson stopped. Walking, thinking, and breathing ceased. It was different when it was someone you loved. A harsh breath sawed against his throat. Detaching was impossible, making it harder and harder to do his job and bring Oliver home. Right now, all his energy channeled into the effort to stay impartial.

Blood. Diluted by the snow, partially covered by the blowing, but unmistakably identifiable. Stark red against a white canvas.

Sweat beaded on his upper lip. A painful rush whooshed deep in his ears. Pain hit his chest. Tiny ice pellets battered his face. No wonder Noah took Kim home. It was too much. More than Jackson wanted to see.

*Don't let it be Oliver's.*

"Noah gave me a rapid blood type test kit. If you know Oliver's blood type, we can see if it's a potential match."

Disorientation and dizziness made it easy for the wind to push him forward. Jackson stumbled. He felt for his phone. *Just do the next thing.*

He called Stuart. Kim shouldn't be back yet, not if Noah stopped by Life House like they had planned, to grab the file she'd started on Elena. Jackson needed the Missing Persons detective to send someone to process the scene, preferably before Kim arrived, so she'd remain unaware.

*Just do the next thing.*

He called Emma. She didn't even say hello. "Did you find Oliver?"

"No, but I need his blood type. Do you have it on file? We're rapid testing a sample. If the type doesn't match Oliver's, Kim never has to know."

"I'll send it to your phone ASAP."

"Thanks. And can you keep this between us?" He wouldn't be able to handle Kim's hysterics. Not when he struggled to hold himself together.

"You bet."

*Just do the next thing.*

Jackson knocked away ice crystals that clung to his whiskers. He squatted, careful not to get too close. Contaminating the evidence helped no one. "Whose do you think it is?"

Simon stood off to the side, giving him time to process. Each retreated to a safe mental place and worked through the potential meanings. They could never unsee this scene. Unfeel these fears. War exposed Simon to the worst of humanity. Jackson arrested men and women who'd committed unimaginable acts. But when it involved a child —it changed a man. This wasn't just any case; it was Oliver.

Deep breath in. Deep breath out.

Oliver, who laughed at all his jokes, cuddled on his lap, and begged for one more story. Oliver looked like

Jackson, because Jackson and Hayden were identical. Strangers addressed Jackson as Oliver's father, and Jackson never corrected them. Deep down, that was what he wanted. He wanted the title, father. Oliver's dad. Kim's husband. And he never quite got over his rotten luck that Hayden met Kim first and screwed it all up.

And now Hayden wanted back in. He'd hinted on the phone that he wanted to make things right with Kim. But what did that mean? Did Hayden want to rekindle their romance? Did he want to apologize? Did he simply want to tell Kim that he was a different man now? If Hayden really was a changed man, he deserved a chance. But none of that would matter if the blood was Oliver's. If Oliver was dead, none of them would ever recover.

*Please, Lord, don't let it be Oliver's.*

Oliver lit up the room with his mischievous grin. He tested Jackson's patience with his endless questions. His boundless energy sent Jackson to bed exhausted.

A low moan grew from the bellows of his soul. Simon turned away. Jackson fell to his knees. One minute. He gave himself one minute to feel, then he stuffed it all into an emotional box and locked it. There'd be time for grief later. When they no longer had hope.

Jackson snorted, stood, and ground his teeth. He swallowed the rising pressure in the back of his throat. Could any pool of blood be victimless? It didn't need to be true, just plausible, so Jackson could continue to hope.

Simon offered a scenario. "If we're lucky, it's animal blood left from some poacher who scored big."

Poachers. Jackson could run with that. The orchards were full of deer.

"But if I had to guess—" Simon pointed at the bush. Tangled in the branches was one of those fabric ponytail holders that girls were always wearing. "Oliver doesn't wear scrunchies and neither do most hunters."

Jackson frowned. Would Kim remember if Elena's hair was up or down? Jackson studied the item's placement in the branches. The thick bush had a small, hollowed-out center. For the hair accessory to get tangled like this, whoever wore it had to have been hiding. He snapped a picture with his phone to show Kim later. "Was she hiding from a pursuer or hiding until a rescuer arrived?"

The tree rustled behind them, sounding more human than animal. The hairs on Jackson's neck prickled. His hand went to his weapon.

"I wouldn't do that if I were you." A coarse, raspy voice, the kind that comes from a heavy smoker, preceded swaying boughs dropping snow. The covering of white slid off the branches and to the ground. Two men decked out in winter camouflage emerged. They pointed their weapons to center mass. One gun levelled at Simon. One gun on Jackson. Jackson didn't like these odds, but then the shorter and stockier one lost his footing and fell to a knee.

"Get up, Damian." The larger man's lips drew back in a snarl.

Damian's pistol barrel slipped under the snow as he found his footing. When he lifted it, snow packed the barrel. That was good. Good for them, at least. Jackson jutted his chin toward Damian. Simon's head jerked. He'd seen it, too.

The gunmen herded Jackson and Simon closer and closer until Simon's back knocked against his. Not the best tactical position.

The big one plucked the scrunchie from the bushes. "She was told no cops. She's gonna pay for that."

They must have seen the cruiser at the house, since Jackson wasn't wearing a uniform. He raised his arms in surrender and took a step toward them. "No one said that. No one said no cops. Not once."

These two were thugs. The mastermind would have known the exact instructions. Even worse, they were amateurs, stumbling around the bush and not noticing a jammed gun barrel. Mistakes made them dangerous and unpredictable.

"I'm not a cop." Simon shifted into a crouch and lowered his voice. "Moving."

The military used terms like moving or cover to communicate tactical posture. Back-to-back was positionally dangerous. Only slightly better than open. Simon would want to get to cover. But before Simon could, Damian aimed the pistol at Simon's chest.

"Then you're no good to us." He pulled the trigger.

Instead of a clean shot, a gunshot combined with the sounds of fracturing metal echoed, drowning Damian's screams.

Simon dove, rolled, and bolted into the trees. Jackson darted in the opposite direction of Simon.

The shooter writhed on the ground. Shrapnel had to be embedded in his skin from the misfire. That made this fight one-to-one. Jackson liked those odds a lot better.

Thrashing behind Jackson confirmed he had the tail. Simon would circle back and contain the shooter. Jackson had to neutralize the thug after him. They'd end this. These two wouldn't hold up under questioning. They'd turn on Nathan.

A shot blasted, and a bullet slammed into a nearby tree. Jackson turtled into his coat as he ran.

Assuming he stayed alive.

# CHAPTER 9

# *11:00 a.m.*

T he hour was nearly up. Kim looked at the front door again. Jackson should be here by now. It was impossible not to read into his absence. He wouldn't miss the kidnappers' phone call unless it had been necessary. Her list of potential reasons for Jackson's delay churned her stomach. What if he found the kidnappers? Or worse, they found him? What if they hurt him? What if Elena returned and brought trouble with her?

Kim shook off the fear that Noah had uncovered something sinister. The list of possibilities was darker and longer than she could handle.

Kim had heard the undertones in their conversation at the farm. But curiosity didn't change that Jackson was right. Kim couldn't stay with him and get the phone to the detective. The detective needed her here, where they could record and analyze the calls. The team from Orillia arrived a little more than five minutes ago. They already set up the equipment. They were Oliver's best hope. That's why she'd gone with Noah without an argument.

"Where's Meg?"

"I ordered her to leave." Detective Marco Burland's mouth set in a hard line.

Stuart's complexion crimsoned.

Detective Burland and three others were at the house setting up when Kim and Noah returned. After introducing himself, Detective Burland introduced the team. Michael Cravey was the IT guy, and the rest were constables: Celeste Bentley, Tim Hibbs, and the negotiator, Ryan Eastwood.

"Meg had someone pick her up. She said something about going to the church, although considering the stunt you two pulled, I should have tossed her in jail." Stuart slapped some papers on the table. His nostrils flared.

Heat shot up the back of Kim's neck. She shifted her gaze to the casc board the unit had set up in the living room, which was just a fancy white board that held pictures, notes, and a map. It reminded her of the murder board used on television shows. But no one called it a murder board. Not yet. Her stomach turned over. *Please, Lord, never.*

They just needed the kidnappers to contact them again.

11:01.

Her heart galloped. Each beat shoved her heart against her bones. The pressure forced the organ to ooze through the small spaces between each rib. "They've never been late before." She gnawed on a fingernail. She hadn't bitten her nails in decades. But between nervous picking and biting, there wasn't a single free edge or cuticle left. She fisted her hand and swung it to her side, bouncing it off her thigh.

"Don't panic." Detective Burland's clipped tone assured her that he'd been down this road before, and he knew how to play the game.

It'd been two and a half hours since they'd taken Oliver. The first three hours were crucial. She'd done her own research. Jackson thought he could keep the statistics from her and shroud everything in hope, but she'd been here before. A parental abduction was different. She hadn't feared for Oliver's life when Hayden had him. Still, the stats were the same. With each move of the second hand, Oliver's chances of a safe return diminished.

Why hadn't they called?

She practised mindfulness. Breathing in, two-three-four. Out, two-three-four. In, two-three-four. Out, two-three-four.

Her heart continued to fight against the boundaries of her ribs. Where was Jackson? Did the kidnappers grab Elena? Is that why they hadn't called? Or did Jackson stay away because he knew Detective Burland and his team had arrived and Burland would sideline him?

Jackson couldn't be on the team. Even Kim understood that. He'd done what he had to do, and he'd done it with excellence. Now they expected him to do what was required in personal cases. Step aside and let an impartial officer take over. But if Jackson didn't return, they couldn't sideline him.

The phone rang.

Kim choked back a sob. Constable Eastwood looked to Burland, who lifted his hand in a gesture that meant wait. The two second delay dragged like hours. Burland barked at Constable Cravey, who was hurrying. His equipment intercepted phone calls and provided secure communications for the teams. He gave Detective Burland a thumbs up, and Burland pointed at Constable Eastwood to answer.

"This is Constable Ryan Eastwood. Who am I speaking with?"

"Where's Kim?"

"She's here. What will it take to get Oliver back?"

Kim gnawed on a fingernail.

"We left Kim a gift at the pond. Don't wait too long. The ice is pretty thin. She should come alone." They disconnected.

Kim's gaze zipped to the detective's. The game had morphed. Why didn't they ask for Elena? Why the pond? Was it Oliver's body? Was she going to find her baby's body because she protected Elena? Panic squeezed her throat. Black spots bounced in her vision.

Then, Officer Bentley was there. She squeezed her

arms and forced eye contact. "Look at me. That's right. Breathe."

The blackness receded.

"You okay?"

Kim nodded, and Officer Bentley let her go.

"Why didn't they ask for anything?"

No one answered. Detective Burland unloaded a truckload of instructions, mobilizing Bentley and Hibbs to go to the pond.

"They said come alone." What if they saw the officers? What if it made them angry? But no one looked at her. Everybody knew what role they played in this production except her.

"Is it Oliver? Is Oliver the gift?" Her breaths shortened until light-headedness made her vision swim again. She grappled for a hold on the chair back. "Is Oliver dead?"

Everybody stopped. They saw her, finally remembering she was in the room.

"We don't know."

Kim found Detective Burland's lower register strangely calming. It grounded her like an anchor. "They said come alone."

"They always do, and they know you won't. Trust me. I've done this more times than I can count." Grey whiskers shadowed his chin and wrinkles deepened the corners of his blue eyes. He reached for her upper arm and gave her a reassuring squeeze. He didn't need her permission. Still, he waited for her to catch up.

What kind of person spent their life doing stuff like this? Her eyes dropped to his hand on her upper arm. His bare ring finger showed his life was a lonely one. The touch grounded her in reality. Was his single state intentional? Did the constant horror of his job sour him on marriage and parenthood? Did he fear bringing more people into their messed-up world? "What about Jackson?"

"Jackson can't be involved now we're here." His face took on a sympathetic look. "You can't go either. It's too dangerous. You're going to stay here with me. Officer Bentley"—the detective nodded to Celeste, who was pulling on Kim's winter coat—"will pretend to be you and pick up the package."

Before Kim could blink, officers Bentley and Hibbs were gone. Disobeying the kidnapper's direct order could backfire. She couldn't do this anymore. "I'm going to lie down for a bit."

Detective Burland narrowed his eyes. "I know what you did last time. I don't want to hear an engine start out there."

She bobbed her head.

Pulling the bedroom door closed, she balled her fists. Before she could even think through her actions, she slid out her bedroom window and sprinted across the backyard. Her cross-country skis were in the shed.

Adrenaline powered her. She yanked her ski jacket off a hook and pulled it on, clipped her boots into place, and glided down the back alley. If she stayed off the main roads, which were still bogged down with snowdrifts, and hugged the running trails, she'd beat the officers to the pond. She had the home court advantage.

She was already crossing the park when the officers pulled into the area earmarked for a new parking lot.

The parking lot sat opposite of the sledding hill. The town couldn't put down gravel until spring, but they plowed the area. Visitors parked on the frozen grass. It prevented congestion on the neighborhood streets.

Kim booked it across the abandoned park.

Bentley called her name, but Kim kept pushing forward.

The pond and the sledding hill were quiet. The storm might have scared off skaters and sledders. But it was more probable they gathered at the church. Even those who rarely attended church would pray for Oliver. Sycamore Hill banded together for the good of their neighbors. Hope infused her. Pastor Owen had checked in once already and assured her the church was bursting at the seams. Her community was fighting for her and Oliver on the unseen battleground where swords clashed, and God's kingdom forced back the darkness.

Kim glided past the billboard that illustrated the vision the town had for the sled and skate park. She'd granted the town permission to use a picture that Ben had taken of Oliver and Jackson. He'd captured Jackson's adoration for Oliver. He beamed at Oliver while supporting Oliver's weight. Oliver focused and poked his tongue out and scrunched his features while trying to skate. His expression of mixed determination, wonder, and delight undid her. The town council scheduled work to begin in the park in the summer. The hope was to have the recreation center completed before winter cycled around again. Would Oliver be here to see it? He'd been so excited to discover the plan included a hockey rink. This was to replace the danger of kids skating on ice that froze and thawed in a regular cycle as the winter temperature fluctuated in extremes.

Freezing air burned her lungs. On the surface of the pond lay hope: a tiny orange heap. The same orange as Oliver's coat.

Kim skidded to a stop. Her breath quickened as she unclipped her skis and darted across the pond without stopping to check the thickness of the ice. The potential danger didn't cross her mind until the voices yelling at her to wait registered. All she could see was the jacket. All she could hear was the kidnapper's command that she collect the gift.

Her. Not Officer Bentley.

She slid to her knees, and a cry rocketed from her. Relief that the coat wasn't covering a dead body and grief that it wasn't covering a live one battled. He wasn't here. She clutched the jacket to her chest and buried her face in the folds of it. Rocking back and forth, she moaned. She couldn't do this anymore. The cycle of hoping and losing hurt too much.

A brown paper envelope fell from the jacket pocket.

She wiped her frozen cheeks, picked it up, and returned to land.

Officer Bentley glared at her. Wordlessly, she held out her hand for the coat and envelope.

Kim hadn't opened it. She could have. In those few moments alone on the ice, she could have torn it open and seen for herself whatever message the kidnappers had left for her. But she feared what might be inside.

Wearing gloves to protect the evidence, Officer Bentley opened the envelope. After flipping through pictures, she shifted so Kim could see them.

Kim reached to take them, and the constable pulled back. "Fingerprints."

Right. Kim squared her shoulders, steeling her insides. But nothing could have prepared her for images of Jackson, bruised and beaten.

His head lolled to the side. He slumped forward on a wooden chair with his hands tied behind his back. Blood trickled from the corner of his slack lips, exposing a bloodied mouth with missing teeth. One eye had swollen shut. A matted red mess clotted in his hair. She couldn't tell if he was dead or alive. She spun and retched, but there was nothing left for her body to expel.

Officer Hibbs positioned himself on Kim's other side. His gazed roamed the park. Was he looking for a shooter? Did he think they were watching?

Kim struggled to regain control. She wiped her lips with the back of her hand and gave Officer Bentley a curt nod. She was ready to hear the message that accompanied the photographs.

"We've got your kid. We've got your lover. Give us the girl or we go live online at noon and stream the cop's painful death. This is your last chance."

Both officers looked hard at her. "Lover?"

Kim fell to her knees. A keening deeper than she'd ever known ripped from her soul.

# CHAPTER 10

# *11:20 a.m.*

J ackson parked the cruiser at the corner of Kim's street. "We'll have to walk from here."

Simon and Colleen followed him as he hurried to Kim's house. Walking was for later, after Oliver came home. Jackson would walk when he and Kim could each hold a little hand and swing Oliver between them. Until then, Jackson had one speed: double-time.

The kidnapper would have called by now. Jackson's gut panged like he'd downed a gallon of milk long past its expiry date. Sharp. Rolling. Explosive.

He eyed the unfamiliar vehicles parked in front of Kim's property. The vice grip squeezing his lungs lessened a little. Detective Burland was really good. Jackson straightened, and his lungs fully inflated for the first time since eight forty-five this morning. They had help.

Jackson took the porch stairs two at a time. Someone had swept the snow off them and sprinkled salt. He reached for the doorknob. It wouldn't be locked. The great room hummed with activity until he crossed the threshold. The buzz silenced. Jackson stopped, and Simon and Colleen stumbled behind him.

A female officer he didn't know questioned Kim. Tears dampened Kim's cheeks, her complexion all blotchy and red.

Sourness shot up his throat. All the hairs on his body jerked to attention. His skin prickled with cold sweat. They were too late. Oliver was dead.

He opened his mouth, but nothing came out. A squeezing in his throat pinched off the air. Sounds echoed, and the people blurred. He lurched toward the back of the nearest chair. Anything to help him stay upright. Oliver was dead, and he hadn't been here. *No, God. No.*

The constable looked up as he stumbled. Her face drained of color, and her eyebrows squished together. Her tight expression confused him. All she said was, "How?"

Detective Burland strode in from the kitchen and pulled up short. "Jackson?"

Kim's head snapped up. The room broke into a cheer and people started talking over one another. Kim let out a harsh breath. Then, with a snort-cry, she launched herself across the room. She flung her arms around his neck and buried her face in his shoulder. Her body heaved with effort, ragged breathing the only sound. For one glorious second, she pressed herself against him.

His body hummed. His hand dropped to her waist and wrapped around her to pull her closer as he buried his face in her hair. She belonged with him.

Her hands uncoiled from behind his neck, and she pulled back to arm's length. Her palms rested on his chest. With a tipped-back head, she dragged her gaze over his face. Then her fingertips skimmed his features, trailing his jawline, prodding his cheeks, caressing the rims of his ears. It was the gentlest and most intimate contact they'd ever shared. It was like she saw him through touch.

"How?"

The skin around Jackson's eyes tightened. Why was Kim acting this way? Her gaze remained fixed on his. He didn't hear a word of the chaos surrounding them. He only had eyes for her. He knew she saw him as more than Oliver's uncle. Every cell in her body communicated it.

Tears dripped from her chin. The warmth of her fingertips and the closeness of her body felt right. A long exhale lifted and lowered her chest. Her hands returned to his neck as she pressed her forehead to his. She locked her fingers behind his head, curling them into his hair. Then her mouth pressed against his. This wasn't the usual cheek peck they'd shared over the months prior. It was not an innocent greeting between family and friends. In the past, his mouth had found her cheek, forehead, and the top of her head, but not the lips. Never the lips. Not when Hayden remained between them.

His arms cinched her closer. Satisfaction grew as the

last piece of himself snapped into place. Kim was his other half. The one bright spot in a devastating day. She made him believe he could do anything. He savored this. Her. The moment, as private as it could be with the Missing Persons unit watching with their mouths hanging open.

Kim pulled back to cup the back of his head with her hands. If she cared about their audience, she didn't show it. She rested her cheek on his shoulder. "I thought you were dead. All I could think was that I had never told you I love you."

She loved him. The declaration landed with the sweetness of a spring rain. She loved him! Then the rest of her sentence registered. "Wait. Dead?" He withdrew far enough to rotate. He looked at the makeshift case board leaning against the wall. Was that a picture of— His stomach heaved again.

"We got these." Detective Burland held out some photographs in a protective bag. The case board held enlarged copies. Burland didn't mention the embrace, but his mouth set in a hard line. Jackson could expect a lecture later for not disclosing the extent of his personal connection to the case. There were reasons cops didn't investigate cases that involved their family members. Reasons Jackson believed logical and necessary until today.

Jackson untangled himself from Kim. "It's Hayden. It has to be."

"Hayden?" Kim's hand flew to her throat, and her fingers splayed out. "Why is he here?"

"We were on the phone when you called." Jackson pushed the butt of one palm against his eyes. He sank onto the couch and clutched the photographs in his other hand. Was it just that morning that he considered sharing his feelings about Kim with his brother? "He's trying to help. He has to be."

Jackson's head spun like one of the theme park rides at the Winter Carnival. The Hayden he knew would never stand in for Jackson like this. Maybe there was something more to his brother's declaration of repentance. Right on the heels of hope played every memory of Hayden claiming to be sorry and begging for forgiveness. It replayed in his mind like an old movie reel. Hayden had sung this song before, but he'd never changed. Not for long.

"I told him not to come. He didn't listen." Disbelief transformed into anger. "He never listens."

Kim perched beside him like a bird ready to fly at the first sign of danger. She nibbled on her lip. "But how did they get Hayden? How did Hayden find Oliver when we can't? Why do they think Hayden is you? What does that mean?" Kim asked question after question, but Jackson couldn't answer them. He put his head in his hands. Either Hayden was part of this and capable of horrors that sickened Jackson's soul, or Hayden was a victim, now at the mercy of whoever had Oliver. He didn't like either option. He wanted a third choice.

Simon spoke from the doorway where he and Colleen waited. "Could it have been Hayden in the truck that we passed on the road? Maybe the guys we saw nabbed him after we left?"

Simon's suggestion made sense. At least with that option, his brother wasn't evil. Just in the wrong place at the wrong time, trying to be what he should have been from day one—a father to Oliver. None of it added up. Hayden had never stepped up to own his responsibilities. He'd spent his life pushing them off onto Jackson. Why would he come back now unless God really did transform his life?

"They think Hayden is you because they don't know you have a twin." Simon ran his right thumb repeatedly over a scar on his left hand.

"You"—Burland pointed at Simon and Colleen— "can't be here."

The fist that had been squeezing Jackson's lungs since Kim first called him returned, juicing him until nothing but pulp remained. If anything happened to Hayden, it would be his fault.

After he and Simon had lost the gunmen in the woods, they hurried Colleen out of the house in case the men circled back to cause trouble. They passed a truck leaving, but Jackson never got a look at the driver.

"And you." Detective Burland gestured at Jackson with his thumb. "Back it up for me. Walk me through what happened."

"Simon is here because he needs to report his interaction with the kidnappers. We brought Colleen, his wife, because we wouldn't leave her alone at the house." Jackson gave Burland a summary of what happened at the farm.

"So, they know you're a cop."

Jackson nodded and jammed his hands in his pockets.

"But what led Hayden to the farm?" Colleen moved closer to Simon, slipping her arm through his.

"The more important question is, did Hayden arrive just as we escaped, and that's why they think they've captured me?" And his brother never corrected them. A spark of hope that his brother had moved from the kingdom of darkness into the kingdom of light relit. It would take a miracle, but God was in the business of miracles.

Burland handed Jackson the note from the pond. "The guy hunting Elena believes having a cop hostage gives him more leverage. Our only advantage is that they don't realize their error."

Kim briefly pinched the bridge of her nose before her fingers slipped down to press against her lips. "Why wouldn't Hayden correct them?"

"Maybe he did correct them, and they didn't believe him. How much traction could a twin theory get with strangers?"

Jackson refused to let Simon's practical response douse the flame. "Maybe it took the focus off Oliver? Maybe they didn't give him the chance." The possibilities rolled off Jackson's tongue. But Hayden didn't have a selfless bone in his body. He never did. Not even as kids. He'd throw Jackson under the bus to save his own skin every time.

Jackson wanted to roar. None of it made any sense. The weight crushed him. How was he supposed to cope without Hayden? Without his twin? How was he supposed to breathe?

The team's voices faded. Jackson retreated to his memories of Hayden and him as boys, playing in the woods, chasing the bad guys, and being the heroes. It looped to the soundtrack of his throbbing heart.

He reached for Kim. Slowly. Uncertain. The tables had turned. He slipped his large hand into her smaller one, welcoming her anchor. It was something solid to cling to before the pain of what-if and could-have-been swallowed him alive.

# 11:30 a.m.

K im squeezed Jackson's hand. His fingers twitched under hers. He was spiraling. Hayden might have been a lot of horrible things, and he may have made a lot of awful choices, but he was still Jackson's brother. His twin brother. The family Jackson turned his back on to prioritize Oliver. Jackson thought he had a lifetime to reconnect with Hayden, but Hayden now measured impending death in minutes. Not years or months. Not even hours. He only had minutes unless they found him.

Kim leaned into Jackson's side. He'd been her strength and anchor for so long. But he was only a man, and could only carry so much before the weight crushed him. It was her turn to be strong. She touched a hand to his heart.

"I got something." Officer Cravey clicked a few buttons on his laptop. All his tech ran through his computer. "I've been analyzing Kim's communications with the kidnappers. We've been focusing on what the kidnapper said. But there was something different in the background this time. Listen." He muted the voice and ran the background noise. Calypso-style music played.

Jackson pulled away from her, listening intently. "It's the carnival music! They're somewhere near the Winter Festival. On Sundays, the music doesn't start until church ends. That's why we didn't hear it earlier."

"Get me a list of everybody connected to that event." Burland set his palms flat on the table. "I want to know who Nathan spoke to."

"Already on it." Bentley spun her laptop around so Burland could see the screen. "I got a list of employees, and Nathan has a cousin running the Ferris Wheel. A Leo Carty."

"Do we know where cousin Leo is staying?"

"In the Sycamore Trailer Park. The entire crew is there."

Kim lifted a shaky hand to her forehead. It was all moving too quickly. In less than ten minutes, the team had mobilized. Before leaving, Officer Bentley paused in front of Kim and Jackson. She looked in Kim's eyes, and for the first time since the Missing Persons unit had arrived, Kim felt seen.

"I'll bring him home," Celeste promised. "My son is Oliver's age."

Kim nodded. She couldn't imagine doing Celeste's job with a small child at home.

Celeste and Jackson exchanged a look that seemed to satisfy Jackson. The team left. They'd be trekking through the backwoods that led to the trailer park any second.

Jackson paced. He repeatedly dragged a hand down his face. A thready muscle in his neck popped. He wanted to be with the team. Even she could see that.

"I should be there."

"We've been over this." Detective Burland didn't even look up from what he was doing. "You two are here with me and Cravey."

"Sorry I'm late." The front door opened, and a man stomped his feet on the mat. "I'm Constable Thurling from the Thames Creek detachment." He pulled off his hat, and a mop of dark hair spilled out. He looked like a teenager.

Jackson extended his hand. "Thanks for coming. The team just left to follow a lead."

"I stopped to help someone on the side of the road. The roads are nasty." Officer Thurling rubbed his hands together. Spying the coffee pot, he gestured to it. "Do you mind?"

"Help yourself." Jackson started pacing again with one hand gripping his other wrist behind his back.

Kim blocked his path. There wasn't anything she could say. She had nothing to offer except to be in this moment with him. This moment that might change everything for both of them. She reached for him. When he didn't resist, she threaded their fingers together. They stood toe to toe, and Jackson tipped his forehead until it pressed against hers. She didn't know why she'd waited so long to let Jackson know how she felt about him.

That wasn't true. She'd feared another error in judgment. Hayden pulled the wool over her eyes and pretended to be honorable when he wasn't. But Jackson was who he said he was. Her heart had known from day one. That first moment when she saw him in the airport security room when he'd brought Oliver back to her proved it. She felt it when he redirected Oliver to her for comfort in those first few highly charged moments. She saw it when he pulled up the tent pegs and moved to Sycamore Hill to be part of their lives. Jackson showed up. Every day. In a million little ways, he showed her he loved her, and she pretended she didn't see. He never pushed for more than she could give, but he accepted whatever affection she offered. Jackson was a good man. She was lucky to have him.

No, that wasn't right either. She was blessed.

Fluttering filled her stomach. That God had blessed her in the middle of this elaborate plan to rescue Oliver and Hayden slammed her. How did blessing and hardship coexist? Yet, here she was. Blessed beyond measure. Filled to overflowing. Trusting what she did not understand. Their eyes locked. Did he feel it too?

He moved to kiss her cheek.

Kim turned toward him. It was the smallest movement. He didn't pull away. Their noses grazed each other. He pressed his lips to hers. A firm connection.

Soft. A warm promise. It was a kiss of hope. They were going to be a family.

*Lord, please save Oliver. Save Hayden.*

Her breath caught. Cold water splashed the moment. Their family included the person who'd hurt her more than anyone else. Her gaze drifted over Jackson's shoulder to the board holding Hayden's pictures. Kim hadn't been able to look at them when she thought they were Jackson. But it wasn't Jackson. That changed things.

Giving Jackson's hand a squeeze, she moved around him for a closer look. Officer Burland had taped the enlarged pictures up one after the other. Why didn't this version of Hayden exist earlier? Where was this self-sacrificing man when they were together? As she looked at the images, she realized she'd forgiven Hayden. Over the last year, she'd moved past the bitterness and found peace. She wanted good things for him and his future. She wanted his relationship with his brother repaired, even if it made her life uncomfortable.

"Don't look at them." Jackson tugged her arm.

She pulled away. "Is that corrugated metal?" Behind Hayden, a wall of sheet metal rippled like waves. It triggered a memory.

"We thought maybe it was the inside of a tractor trailer." Burland crossed the room and stood beside her as she studied the images. "Cravey is tracking shipments and looking for recent sales. Nathan's cousin might be in a trailer converted to a camper."

Warmth buzzed in her chest. Her hair swayed as she shook her head. "No, it's not a trailer. It's a shelter." Kim dragged her fingertips over the map tacked to the board. She knew this place. She knew where Hayden was, and it wasn't the fairgrounds. "Oliver and I were here when they took him." She pointed at a mark on the map at the abduction site. "We were going to church, which is here." She stuck a magnetic pin to the church's location.

Jackson tucked his hands under his armpits as he joined them. A furrow deepened between his eyebrows. "They'd have to be local to grab Hayden, take those pictures, and drop them at the pond."

"The pond is here." Kim pointed to a third location, marking it with another pin. "Add Willow Creek Farms." She pulled her bottom lip into her mouth. She was right. It was the only place that made sense.

"What are you thinking?" The side of Jackson's arm brushed against hers.

Her gazed roamed the map. She appreciated no one commented on the ticking clock. They waited, letting her think, letting her gather her thoughts. If she was wrong and they diverted officers from saving Oliver . . . But if she didn't suggest it, if she were right and Oliver or Hayden died because of it . . .

She couldn't finish that thought, either.

The tip of her tongue pushed against the back of her teeth. "It's only a guess. Maybe I'm crazy." She moved to her bookcases and ran the pad of her index finger along the spines of the novels and books she'd collected over the years. She pulled out a photo album. It was the old kind that had plastic sheets that you peeled back so you could tuck the photographs underneath. She flipped through the pages. "Is it just me, or does the wall behind Hayden look like this?"

The picture was of herself with her dad in front of a metal corrugated wall. It was identical to the wall behind Hayden, right down to the same scratch mark across the middle.

Jackson held the album against the picture of Hayden. "Where is this?"

"It's on the property my great-grandfather used to own. It's an old bomb shelter set back from the hiking trails, and it's near the fairgrounds." She stuck two pins onto the map. "Here's the shelter and the fairground."

"They're central to the other places."

"A bomb shelter?" Burland spun and slapped the table with both hands. "Why didn't anyone know about the bomb shelter?"

Thurling jumped, spilling his coffee, and Cravey pounded the laptop keys, pulling up information.

Kim hugged herself. "It's not common knowledge. My great-grandfather built it after the war. I only saw it once. It had fallen into such disrepair that it wasn't safe. Dad showed me when I was writing a paper in high school about the impact of the war on small towns. The area is so overgrown. I'm not even sure I could find it again."

"How much time do we have?" Officer Thurling looked at his watch.

"Twenty minutes."

Kim pressed a fist to her mouth. Twenty minutes. It wasn't enough time. "I should have looked sooner."

Jackson crushed her in an embrace. He squeezed her against his chest so hard she could barely breathe. His bristly cheek rubbed her temple. His lips warmed her ear. "You did it. You found him."

"I got information on the shelter." Cravey's fingers clicked on the keyboard. "Sending the location to your devices now."

"Jackson, you and Thurling head to the shelter. I need Bentley and Hibbs to stay on Oliver."

"Take this." Cravey handed Thurling an earpiece. "We'll keep you in the loop about the exchange."

"What about me?" Kim's mouth dried up.

"You're staying put. You and Officer Eastwood have a phone call to answer."

Kim swallowed. Right. The negotiator. She lifted her gaze to Jackson.

He cupped her hands with his and leaned in. "You can do this. We're going to get our family back."

CHAPTER 12

# Noon

J ackson swatted a low-hanging branch from his face. Thurling had parked the cruiser a distance away, and now they hiked in. Their winter camouflage helped them blend into their surroundings.

"We've found the shelter." Thurling updated Burland through his com.

Thurling had less experience than Jackson. He was greener than the grass after a spring rain. Yet Thurling wore the com because Jackson wasn't supposed to be working the case.

Thurling's brow furrowed as he focused on the voice in his ear.

Jackson hated he didn't have an earpiece. He hated depending on Thurling to relay updates. He got it. He understood why it was this way. Still, he didn't like it.

Thurling signaled Jackson. "The exchange is going down. As soon as they have Oliver, we'll breach."

This was it. It would be over in a few minutes. Jackson rolled his shoulders. *Please, Lord. Please.*

Kim remained at the house with Burland and Eastwood. She had to be going crazy, but she'd be okay. She was strong. Jackson had first admired Kim's strength when he reunited her with Oliver a little more than a year ago. She'd shown great restraint in her movements. Despite aching with agony, wanting to hold Oliver, hug him, and cling to him and never let go, she held back. She'd suffered in ways most parents would never know, but she waited for Oliver's invitation. Putting her son's needs above her own, she waited until Oliver was ready.

Then she welcomed Jackson and his parents into her life. She accepted them, even after all Hayden had put her through and months of separation from Oliver and the agony of not knowing where her son was. And when she learned that Oliver's grandparents had him, she never blamed them. She accepted and believed that they didn't know Hayden had kidnapped his child. Her strength was beautiful.

She would do everything she could to save Oliver, except trade a soul for a soul. Not even to save her child. That took an uncommon strength. Supernatural strength. It came from a deep trust in God. *Lord, bless her desire to honor all life.*

Jackson's insides throbbed. His fingertips vibrated. Hayden and Oliver were close. The faint music from the carnival provided distant background noise. The shelter was underneath his feet. Nathan would be at the exchange. But he'd have left some muscle to guard Hayden.

"They're walking Bentley to the exchange point." Thurling cupped a hand over his ear, listening intently. "They see Oliver."

Jackson crept closer to the shelter's opening. According to Cravey's research, the shelter had two entrance points. It had a hatch in the top and a tunnel in the side of a hill. Kim confirmed only the tunnel was functional when she and her dad visited.

A figure with a bandaged hand emerged.

Jackson snorted. Damian. The misfired pistol hadn't taken the sloppy gunman out of commission.

The radio on Damian's hip buzzed. A second man wandered out, gesturing with his gun. Jackson's gut clenched. There was nothing blocking the barrel of that gun.

*Whatever happens, Lord, save Oliver.*

Thurling's expression contorted. Something had gone wrong with the exchange.

"We gotta breach. Go, go, go!" Thurling led, gun drawn. "This is the police. Put your weapon on the ground and your hands in the air."

The larger man spun, lifting his gun, and Thurling squeezed the trigger.

The man dropped.

Damian thrust his hands upward as Jackson approached. "Do you have a weapon?"

"A gun in my waistband."

"I got it." Thurling secured the first man, then lifted the back of Damian's jacket and removed the gun.

Jackson tossed Thurling his cuffs, keeping his weapon trained on Damian. Thurling secured him.

"You got him?"

Jackson nodded.

Thurling disappeared into the shelter. Seconds later, he emerged from the tunnel with an arm around Hayden.

"They have a second car hidden at the south entrance to the campgrounds." Dried blood covered Hayden's face. One eye had swollen so much only a slit remained. He was alive, and to Jackson, he'd never looked better. "Nathan was going to the backup vehicle if anything went wrong."

"We'll secure the prisoners and head to Sour Springs Road." Thurling relayed their movements through his com. "Let's go." He nudged the cuffed men in the cruiser's direction.

"You'll never get there in time." An ugly laugh peeled from Damian.

Thurling prodded his back.

Hayden grabbed Jackson's shoulder. "They have snowmobiles. I saw where they put the keys."

Jackson met Thurling's eyes. "Plan B?"

Thurling's chin lifted. "Hayden, grab the keys. Jackson, you get the spike strip."

By the time Jackson grabbed the spike strip from the cruiser's trunk, Hayden had the snowmobile running.

The twins faced each other. Jackson didn't like the rattle in his brother's chest.

"Go." Hayden's mouth twisted. It would have been a smile if his face hadn't pinched. He rubbed a bloodied hand across his jaw. "Get Oliver back."

"Lord willing, Officer Bentley already has him. She has a son the same age." That similarity would drive Bentley. Celeste would bring Oliver home or die trying.

Hayden blew out his cheeks and winced.

"Constable Thurling will bring you."

"I know."

Jackson secured the spike strip to the back of the snowmobile.

"I'll see you there." Hayden rubbed a hand over his chest and tapped his heart twice. It was the secret signal they used as kids.

"I love you, too." Jackson choked back emotion.

Seconds later, he flew over the fields. Avoiding the main roads saved significant time. He had to beat Nathan to Sour Springs Road.

Encouraged by the undisturbed snow, Jackson hopped off the snowmobile and grabbed the spike strip. He tossed it across the road just as the roar of an engine grew in volume.

A black SUV took the bend way too fast. Its back end slid. The vehicle hit the spikes. Jackson retracted the strip as the SUV skidded to an anticlimactic stop. All four doors opened, and several figures emerged like an exploded ant farm.

"Police. Put your hands up!" Jackson leveled his gun at the men.

Thurling's cruiser approached from the other side.

A streak screamed across the field.

*Oliver!*

Oliver's little legs pumped. He didn't have a jacket. Tears and dirt stained his cheeks. But he was alive.

"Gun!"

The gunman swung toward Thurling's roar, and Hayden launched himself toward Oliver.

Jackson swiveled to cover his brother. He didn't have a shot. "Get down!"

Thurling fired.

It wasn't supposed to go this way. This wasn't the plan.

Bodies and bullets spilled into the clearing. But all Jackson saw was the terrified boy running.

*Take me instead, Lord.*

Everything went too slow and too fast at the same time. The speeds battled in Jackson's brain for dominance. He just needed to reach Oliver. He had to get to Oliver.

But Hayden beat him.

Hayden dove and knocked Oliver to the ground with the cry of a warrior. He covered Oliver's body with his.

Jackson skidded to them and positioned himself on one knee. He held his gun over their cowering bodies and picked off armed men as they emerged like some warped game of Whack a Mole. Officers Bentley and Hibbs blocked the exit and joined the fight. Who would emerge as the victor was not the question. The good guys had this. The real question was how many casualties would such a victory cost?

*Please, Lord.*

Hayden and Oliver were too quiet.

Jackson reached for a pulse. Hayden turned to him. He opened his mouth as if he were about to speak as a shadow rose in front of them.

"Jackson!" Hayden charged like a bull on fire. He rammed the gunman at full tilt just as the gun went off. Both bodies hit the snow-covered ground and rolled.

Jackson pounced on the fallen man and wrenched his hands behind his back, making him howl. He bound his wrists to immobilize him.

Hayden rolled. Red bubbled through his fingers. A shot had pierced his shoulder.

"Looks like a through and through." Jackson put his hands over Hayden and pressed. "Keep pressure on it."

Oliver crawled toward them.

"I'm okay." Hayden's mouth fell open. The adrenaline that rushed through his veins would keep the pain at bay for a few seconds. Maybe minutes. Hayden curled an arm around Oliver and flattened him to the ground.

"Stay down." Chaos continued to abound, but the good guys were taking ground.

Officer Bentley made her way toward them, reached a hand out to Jackson, her eyes fixed on Oliver. A figure emerged behind her. A gunshot exploded as Hayden threw himself toward her, taking her down.

Jackson pulled his trigger and the gunman dropped, a red dot expanding on his chest. "Officer down!" Jackson lunged toward Bentley and Hayden.

Bentley rolled out from underneath Hayden. "I'm not hit."

Hayden's body jerked. A sudden stiffening posture. His eyes widened further, and then his features slackened. A stain seeped through his clothing near his heart. The surprised look in his eyes dulled.

"Hayden!" Jackson's chest constricted.

Everything faded as a wail grew. The wailing increased until it was all Jackson heard because it came from inside of him.

# CHAPTER 13

*12:15 p.m.*

K im saw Emma first, and she ran to her friend. Before she could speak, Emma answered. "They're fine. Oliver and Jackson are fine."

Kim collapsed into Emma's arms, and Emma rocked her slowly. "I'll take you to them."

They threaded through the chaos. Kim could barely register the scene. Cloths covered three bodies. Dead, she assumed. People with badges and official uniforms of all kinds swarmed the area. Kim's gaze skimmed it all, finding none of what she was looking for.

"Mommy!"

Her heart lurched.

Oliver wiggled free from Constable Bentley and threw himself at her. Kim fell to her knees and opened her arms. She pulled Oliver close, pressed her nose to his sweaty head, and cried. Her chest swelled.

Oliver didn't have his coat. Officer Bentley had slung her larger jacket over his shoulders. He looked like a kid playing dress-up. The cold registered as dampness seeped through Kim's jeans, but she stayed where she was. She didn't trust her legs to stand. Everywhere she looked magnified the cost of Oliver's rescue. Blood stained the snow.

"Kim?" Emma touched her shoulder. "Let me take Oliver."

Kim swung him out of reach and tightened her hold.

Emma crouched in front of her and looked her dead in the eyes. "Jackson needs you, and you don't want Oliver to see this." Emma tipped her head toward Jackson's direction.

Jackson and Matt hovered over a body prone on the ground. Matt crouched over the man, his army field training hard at work. Matt had performed emergency procedures while overseas. He'd know what to do while they waited for an ambulance from Grander. Matt pressed both hands over the chest wound, but thick red oozed between his fingers. "I'm losing him!"

"Not Unca Jackson," Oliver said. "Not Unca Jackson." His chant broke through the roar in Kim's ears.

*Hayden.*

"You're right. It's not Uncle Jackson." She stroked Oliver's silky hair, pushing it back off his forehead. He looked just like he had this morning. Perfect. Her tears dripped off her chin. She dragged her jacket sleeve across of her face. Her son. She had him back. He was okay. The impossibility of it made her bones quiver. She ran her hands down his arms and legs. She brushed her fingertips over his facial features. He was fine. She couldn't believe it. He was fine.

"I need to help Uncle Jackson. Can you stay with Emma? She'll stand close enough that you can see me the whole time."

Oliver peered into her eyes. "It's not Unca Jackson, Mommy. It's Unca Hayden."

*Uncle Hayden?* Why would Hayden tell Oliver that he was his uncle?

"Unca Hayden found me. He said I go home soon."

A sob swelled in her throat. Kim pulled Oliver into her arms and pressed his cheek against her shoulder. She stood and handed him to Emma. Jackson needed her.

The desperation in Matt's movements increased the pressure behind Kim's eyes. No matter what Hayden had done in the past, no matter how many ways and how many times he disappointed his brother, hurt her, or manipulated Oliver, he was still Jackson's brother. His only brother. His twin. The other half of him. You couldn't break that kind of bond. It couldn't end like this.

"Jackson?"

Jackson's lips moved, but his words didn't register. It was like she floated above the chaos, detached from the scene, watching it unfold from a safe distance. She saw

Emma holding Oliver, his tear-streaked face pressed into her body and his tiny fingers clutching the fabric of her jacket. The other officers cuffed and hauled men to their feet. Jackson crouched on his knees, his face close to his brother's, lips moving, hands working. This wasn't the ending Kim would have scripted. But really, she didn't know how she'd write the end.

Her heart belonged to Jackson, but her body was one with Hayden. Two fleshes had joined. She didn't need her signature on a marriage certificate for that truth to hold weight in her soul. As broken as they were, Hayden was a part of her. He'd always be a part of her. God used Hayden to shape her into the woman she was today, to sand her edges, to make her more like Jesus.

But when Hayden traded himself for Oliver and Jackson, it was so out of character she didn't have a mental compartment for the action. She'd only known him to put himself first. Leaving him was the hardest thing she'd ever done. The scariest. It drove her to start Life House. It was why she came alongside people like Elena. She knew.

It took courage to stand up to a bully, and Kim knew what it cost to protect a child. She knew how it felt when someone took that child away, and she knew what it meant to only have God and to struggle to believe that He was good.

Red seeped from under Hayden's body and into the precipitation. It spread out in a ring underneath him. His eyes were open, staring into the sky as huge flakes of white clung to his eyebrows. The man who'd brought her unspeakable pain fought for each breath.

Kim dropped beside Jackson. The former chaos settled into a tense and screaming silence. The rescue hadn't gone as planned. Hayden had been shot.

"What were you thinking?" Jackson squeezed Hayden's hand.

Hayden turned toward Jackson's voice. They locked eyes. A lifetime replayed. Kim got the feeling that forgiveness had been asked for and granted without a word whispered.

Burland shoved medical pads under Matt's hands.

"I couldn't let her die." Hayden coughed. "She has a kid like Oliver. You said so. A kid needs his mother."

Hayden did this on purpose? Kim's head swirled.

"All the things you said . . ." Jackson's voice cracked as Matt pressed the pads over the wounds. "Your new faith, your desire to make amends . . ." Jackson choked, an anguished and tormented sound. "I'm sorry. I should have believed you. I do believe you."

The white absorbent pads turned red. Heat scorched the back of Kim's eyes. They were saying goodbye. *No, Lord. This is not how it ends.*

"I never gave you a reason to believe." Hayden coughed again. He turned his head to the side and spat out blood.

Burland spoke into the radio on his shoulder. Kim

didn't hear his words, but she didn't need to hear them to understand his expression.

She glanced back at Emma and Oliver. A part of her wanted to walk away. It told her to scoop up her child and leave, giving the brothers this moment, but she couldn't. It was like cement had filled her limbs and she was stuck in this spot watching her past and her present collide with spectacular grief. Never in a million years did she ever think the three of them would find themselves in a circumstance where she'd be rooting for Hayden. Not when his presence threatened the future she wanted.

Yet, here they were. And with everything in her, she wanted him to live. She wanted him and Jackson to have time to make new memories. She wanted Oliver to know how Hayden showed up when it mattered. How the two men most connected to him in this world nearly gave their lives for his. She didn't just want Oliver to hear the story from her lips; she wanted him to hear the story told from them, healed and restored. Even if it meant she and Jackson could never be together. Even if it meant the consequence of her choices all those years ago was to trust the Lord with her future and with her heart. There was no fairytale end to this story. No happily-ever-after. It was too messy. Too many shades of grey. Too many layers of grief.

"You didn't have to do this." Jackson's mouth tightened. His lips turned white.

"It had to be me. Her kid needs her. And Oliver

shouldn't lose his father." Hayden wheezed and coughed some more.

"You're Oliver's father."

"No." Hayden spoke so firmly that Matt's hands paused. Hayden's eyes cleared, and he held Jackson's gaze. "I'm the seed. You're the father."

Hayden's eyes clouded over again. They shifted and found her. Kim couldn't hold back her tears.

"I'm sorry." His face pinched as if every agonizing breath shredded his insides.

"I can't believe you came." She grazed her fingertips down his cheek.

"Of course, I came." His eyes squeezed closed. "It was you. It was Oliver."

Kim's breathing grew raspy. This couldn't be the end.

"Do you love him?"

She hiccupped a breath.

"Jackson. Do you love him?" Hayden repeated.

Jackson froze. Kim felt lightheaded. She didn't want to hurt Hayden, but she couldn't lie. "I do."

Hayden nodded. The movement was slight, like it cost him a lot to make it. "He's better than me. You have my blessing."

"You're going to be fine." Kim choked.

"I'm sorry for everything."

She'd heard those words a million times in the past. He was always sorry, but he never changed. He reverted to old patterns every time.

"I believe you." She pressed a gentle kiss to his forehead. "And I forgive you."

The tension left Hayden's face. As his features relaxed and the hardness in his body softened, Kim saw the man she'd loved years ago. She saw him for the choice he'd made in this moment—to put their child first no matter the personal cost. And she loved him for it.

It took hours to clean up the scene. More police officers arrived from other detachments, and Emma treated the wounded as best she could before the ambulances arrived from the city.

Kim sat with Oliver on her lap, fully believing that she would never let him go ever again. For now, he seemed content to let her hold him. Matt had done what he could for Hayden like he'd done for fellow soldiers in the war. After their brief interaction, Hayden passed out. Matt could not rouse him again. There was nothing left to do but pray.

Kim updated Pastor Owen and Gloria, who passed the information to the congregation. They'd been praying since nine o'clock in the morning, gathered in the church sanctuary doing battle on the unseen field. They promised to keep praying for Hayden's recovery.

The paramedics loaded Hayden into the ambulance. The medics didn't look optimistic as they slammed the ambulance's bay doors. Jackson pressed a kiss to Kim's forehead and another one on Oliver's cheek and went with his brother.

One question remained. It swirled in the aftermath's chaos—a mystery yet to be solved. Round and round it went in her head. She wanted it to stop. For the puzzle to be complete. But they were still missing a few pieces to the story. Where was Elena? And why did Hayden go to the farm in the first place?

# CHAPTER 14

# March - One Month Later

J ackson couldn't take his eyes off Oliver. He played on the floor in Kim's now-cleaned up living room. No physical evidence of the former command center remained. Emotional evidence? That was a different story.

Oliver's footie pajamas stretched over his body like a second skin. His hair, damp from a bath, was combed off his face. His little lips puckered as he fit wooden train tracks together that spanned the length of the couch. He pushed a red train, making muffled noises. His cheeks puffed out with each chug of the engine, and Jackson's chest tightened. He wasn't sure if the stress in his body would ever fully release. They'd nearly lost him.

Beams from a vehicle's headlights arched through the picture window. The curtains were open despite darkness descending over an hour ago. Kim's neighbour backed her vehicle out of the driveway and drove down the street. To anyone peeking in from the outside, they looked like a family. A husband and wife puttering around the house. A fire glowing in the fireplace and the toddler playing on the carpet while the snow blew outside, frosting the windows. Dishes clanked in the kitchen, where Kim finished drying and putting away the plates Jackson had washed. To anyone looking in, they seemed normal. Typical. Functional.

Looks were deceiving on so many fronts.

Oliver, still clingy since his abduction, was restless after his bath. He insisted that someone sit in the living room with him. He was unsatisfied with playing in the kitchen and didn't want to wait for the dishes to be put away. He didn't want to be alone. Oliver didn't know what he wanted, but he knew what he didn't want. Kim nudged Jackson to go with Oliver, insisting that she would finish cleaning up.

"Play?" Oliver lifted a second train and handed it to Jackson. The tightness in Jackson's face lessened. He moved to the floor, sat on the opposite side of the train tracks as Oliver, and pushed the green engine down the rails. The magnets on the train cars were not strong enough for Jackson to pull the long train Oliver had clicked together. It separated in the middle.

He couldn't believe it had already been a month since Oliver's kidnapping. Hayden lingered on life support long enough for Jackson's parents to fly in and say good-bye. Jackson could have never guessed how one Sunday morning would change everything for everyone. Especially for Oliver, who drove his train along the track, unaware of the cataclysmic shifts that had occurred in his world.

Strangers assumed Oliver was Jackson's son. They shared the same skin tone and eye color. Their hair curled in the same backward wave that drove Jackson nuts. Their biological connection was obvious. But Oliver was Hayden's child. And now, Oliver would never know his birth father.

An ache unlike any other filled Jackson's soul like it did every time he thought of Hayden and his final sacrificial acts. Pressure built behind his eyes, and he scrubbed a hand down his face.

Oliver looked up, studied Jackson for a minute, and looked at the broken train. "I help." Oliver clicked the magnet on the front of his engine to the magnet on the abandoned cars. He chugged along behind Jackson. "All fixed."

Jackson's pulse throbbed in his throat. "Thanks, buddy."

Jackson couldn't excuse all the choices his brother had made in life. He couldn't pretend to be okay with the shady lifestyle he'd led or the way he flirted with the law and hurt the people who loved him. But that didn't mean Jackson wanted to lose him. It didn't make Hayden's death easier.

"I be a good helper."

"You're a great helper." When Hayden died, so did a part of Jackson. For a while, Jackson believed the part of him connected to his twin was gone forever. But he'd come to see that Oliver was a part of Hayden. Oliver was the piece that lived on and was the best part of his brother.

Kim coughed, and Jackson's head snapped up. She leaned a shoulder against the doorframe of the kitchen and watched them. Her eyes glazed, damp and gentle. "Coffee?"

"Yes, please."

She disappeared into the kitchen.

Jackson slipped his hand into his front pocket and fingered the family heirloom that begged to be slipped onto Kim's finger. He'd carried it with him all week, waiting for the perfect moment to make them everything they weren't yet: an actual family. "I'm going to sit on the couch." Jackson pushed himself off the floor. "Do you want to snuggle with me or play trains?"

"Trains." Oliver didn't even look up.

Jackson moved on the sofa so there was room for Kim. He rubbed a palm over his gut. Tension, he could do. Fear? All in a day's work. Horror? Not his favourite part of his job, but it came with the territory. Romance? Love? Making a relationship permanent? Becoming a dad? That was new.

Hayden had given his blessing before he died, shoving Jackson over the platonic line that had held him back all year. But how long was a guy who'd been waiting his whole life for a woman like Kim supposed to wait in a situation like this? Was there a grieving period?

His parents told him to go for it. His mom twisted grandma's ring off her finger and pressed it into Jackson's palm. If Hayden were here, he'd kick Jackson and say, get to it.

But this might not be an option if Hayden were here.

Jackson knew acutely that his shot at happiness with Kim came at the cost of Hayden's life. It was a lot to process. For him. For her. For everyone. Was she ready for it?

The sofa cushion sagged as Kim joined him and pressed a steaming mug into his hand. She cradled hers as she gazed at Oliver.

He hoped so. He was about to change their entire future if she said yes.

She'd say yes.

Oliver put his train down, pushed himself to his feet, gave Jackson's legs a hug, kissed Jackson's knee, repeated the gestures with his mom, and then returned to the toys. He'd been doing little things like that all month with Kim. Kim had asked Emma about it, and she'd insisted it was normal. Feeling overwhelmed and seeking his mom was a part of Oliver's processing. It made him feel safe again.

This was the first time he'd done it with Jackson.

He felt— Well, he didn't know how he felt. Knowing his presence made Oliver feel safe made his insides swell. A month ago, he wasn't sure what the next step was, but together, they'd grieved for what could have been, what should have been, but never would be. He and Kim faced the worst a couple could face and came out stronger. They belonged together.

There would be nights of dreams, tears, and terror as Oliver's young mind processed everything he endured. The body would force the trauma to the surface. Kim would process all she nearly lost, and all she did lose. But as they did, Jackson would be there to help. They'd do it together.

Jackson slung an arm around her shoulders, and she curled into his side. His body was exhausted, yet he doubted either of them would get much sleep, and it would have nothing to do with the caffeinated beverages they sipped.

Kim curled her legs underneath her and tugged a knitted throw blanket over her lower half. Oliver got up and stood in front of her on his tiptoes, trying to see into her mug. "Hot chocolate?"

"No." She covered the top of the mug with her hand. "Coffee." She made a funny face.

Oliver mimicked her expression and returned to his toys. "Coffee yucky."

Jackson enjoyed the normalcy of the moment. A tiredness that was more fulfilling than exhausting filled him. "Have you heard anymore from Burland?"

"Yes. He said Nathan's cousin got my cell number from my electronic ticket purchase to the Winter Festival. That's how they knew what number to video call."

"That makes sense." The puzzle pieces had filled in

throughout the last four weeks. They even figured out why Hayden had gone to the farm.

After Meg lent her car to Kim, enabling Kim to follow him to Willow Creek Farm, Detective Burland had sent Meg home. Meg called Gloria for a ride to the church, so she could join the prayer meeting. As she waited for Gloria to pick her up, Hayden arrived. Meg thought Hayden was Jackson and started apologizing for interfering before Hayden could speak, and Hayden didn't correct her. She asked how it went at Willow Creek Farm, and he made up some excuse and left.

"Will you get to see Elena?"

Kim shook her head. "The police moved her into protective custody until after Nathan's hearing. She needs to testify, but Burland is passing my messages along."

"You really impressed him when you remembered that Elena wore a fitness watch and asked if he could ping it to track her down."

Kim lifted one shoulder in a shrug. "I used to watch a lot of crime shows."

Jackson laughed at her use of the past tense. The only programs they'd watched since Oliver's return were kids' shows or lighthearted comedies. They'd had enough crime for a lifetime. "I'm glad Elena is safe."

"And so is her baby. Nathan won't be able to touch them ever again. That's all that matters."

Elena was clever. Even Jackson had been impressed. She had run to a friend's house in Grander when Quinn messaged the code for trouble was coming. That Kim never forgot that in the middle of her nightmare with Oliver, another mother was fighting for her baby's life as well, made Jackson love her more.

Jackson took a long drink of coffee. The velvety liquid soothed his throat. "It kills me that Oliver will never know Hayden." Would Kim have given Hayden another chance so Oliver might know his dad? Did Hayden's death stain their relationship in a way that tarnished it forever?

Kim lowered her gaze to her cup. Her finger dragged along the rim. "I know." She lifted her face. "I know Hayden was changed because the Hayden I remembered would have never done the things he did for Celeste, Oliver, or for you."

Enough for her to grieve Hayden? Enough for her to need more time?

She repositioned herself.

This was it. His moment. His heart hammered in his chest.

She brought the mug to her lips again and waited. She lifted her eyebrows in a question. He couldn't tell what she was thinking, but her forehead crinkled in the most adorable way. They hadn't discussed her earlier declaration of love. They hadn't kissed again since the day Hayden had died. Did she regret it? Would she try to deny it or try to explain her reaction away? No matter what she did, she couldn't pretend she wasn't driven by love.

And not an extended-family kind of love. This was the love he'd been waiting for. It involved risk. Danger. It was costly. Knowing she loved him didn't guarantee that she'd accept his proposal. She'd already proven that she could make hard choices when necessary. She'd already shown her character. Obedience to God mattered more than desires.

He took a breath. *Lord, if this is Your will, if this is good for her, for us, help her see it and not feel guilt.*

He set his mug on the end table and slipped off the sofa and onto one knee.

Oliver stopped playing and looked up. Kim's hands trembled. Coffee sloshed onto the fabric of the sofa. Jackson took the mug from her and set it beside his. He wrapped both her unsteady hands in his. Unable to read her expression, he plowed forward anyway.

"I've loved you since the moment I met you. I love your love for God, your sense of justice, your selfless heart. There were a million reasons I couldn't ask you this question before, but none of those reasons remain."

Jackson slipped his hand into his pocket and pulled out the ring.

# CHAPTER 15

*May - Two Months Later*

"Oliver!" Kim tapped her heeled foot on the hardwood floor at the bottom of the short staircase. If he didn't hurry, they'd be late. The crash and thud that came from inside his bedroom made her smile. He was probably looking for his bunny. Her eyes prickled. She pressed her fingers against them until the pressure subsided. He got his dramatic flair from his father.

An ache swelled in her chest. She swallowed and tightened her grip on the banister. Hayden wouldn't be there today. Her midsection flip-flopped.

At her wedding.

"Oli-verrrr!"

Oliver popped through his bedroom doorway and into the hallway. She smiled as he bounded down the stairs.

She wiggled his bunny. "Look what I have."

He skidded to a stop in front of her and tugged the

bunny to his chest with a squeal. The rabbit's ears flopped. Oliver lifted his face.

She bent and kissed his cheek, fingering the collar of his suit jacket. "You look sharp."

"I so sharp I could cut you." He puffed out his chest.

Jackson's parents followed Oliver down the stairs. "Sorry it took so long." Mr. McGregor ruffled his grandson's hair. "He's a squirmy little fella. That tie was tricky." The adoring look in their eyes made Kim think she might burst. Mr. and Mrs. McGregor were a special couple.

"Tricky." Oliver beamed at his grandfather.

"Are you ready?" Kim's mom came inside from the front porch. Her long skirt swirled around her ankles, and her eyes sparkled when they landed on Kim. "You look stunning."

Kim gave a little twirl. "I feel like a princess."

"Prettier than a princess." Her mom's fingertips moved lightly over her heart. "Your dad's in the van. He picked up Meg and Emma."

A gentle wind rocked the branches of the nearby Sycamore tree and kissed their cheeks as they trudged to the car. The scent of pine from the trees lining the property intensified. Emma hopped from the passenger side of the van and opened the door for Kim.

It took at least five minutes to tuck the layers and layers of tulle that made up her dress into the vehicle. Jackson's dad leaned forward to speak to Oliver through the open side door. They fist bumped. "Nana and I will follow in our car. See you there, champ." He nodded at Kim's dad, who was behind the wheel.

After much laughing, and ensuring Oliver was buckled properly, they were off. Twelve-thirty. Not too bad. The ceremony was supposed to start at one o'clock.

Dad turned on the Christian radio station. A familiar tune about God's ability to bring beauty from ashes made Kim's cheeks warm. Three months ago, she wouldn't have thought that even God could redeem all that had gone wrong. But today— She blinked fast.

"If you cry, you'll ruin your makeup." Emma extended the tissue box.

Kim dabbed her eyes. "I'm fine. It's just a bit over-whelming."

Oliver chattered to himself. He held the bunny up to the window. "See Unca Jackson?"

"We'll see him at church."

Emma took a couple of tissues and stuffed them into her tiny clutch. "Are you ready? Gloria is at the church. She said Kathryn is all set up to capture our arrival on film."

Kim massaged the muscles in the back of her neck, then shook out her tingling hands. In a little more than an hour, she'd be Jackson's wife. "I'm ready."

"I ready, too!" Oliver chirped.

They arrived at the church, and with much laughter and fun, they made their way into the foyer. Kathryn snapped dozens of photographs before letting the camera drop and embracing Kim. "I'm so happy for you."

"Thank you." Kim sniffed back a tear and leaned into the embrace of her friend. It had taken so much to get to this moment with Jackson.

The double doors leading into the sanctuary were closed. Jackson was on the other side. Jackson waited at the end of the aisle for her to walk toward him and promise forever.

Mrs. Brisbane, Meg's neighbor, organized them into a line. She oohed and aahed over Kim as she ensured Kim's father stood on the proper side and that they were out of sight when the ushers opened the doors to escort her mom and Jackson's parents to their seats at the front.

This was it. The wedding party was next.

The exterior doors whooshed. A blushing guest dipped her head with an apology. As she scurried past, Gloria gasped. "Tiffany?"

Mrs. Brisbane clucked her tongue and steered Tiffany by her elbow into the sanctuary.

Kim only knew of one Tiffany that could pull this kind of reaction from her friend. This was the former university roommate that tried to frame Gloria. The woman who jeopardized the Life House residents with some bogus drug study. Why on earth would she crash her wedding?

"We don't have time for this." Gloria smoothed her hands down the front of her dress. "We can deal with it later."

"But—"

"No buts." Mrs. Brisbane clapped her hands together upon her return. "That's your cue, ladies."

The doors to the sanctuary swung open. Oliver made a move, and Kim pulled him back. "Not yet."

The girls walked single file in a slow procession. A groomsman met each bridesmaid mid-aisle and escorted her the rest of the way. Now it was Oliver's turn. She squeezed his shoulders before releasing him. "Walk to Uncle Jackson."

"Look at me, Unca Jackson. I'm just like you!" Oliver gave a little spin before he raced down the aisle.

The guests laughed, and all eyes turned to Kim. It took all her self-control to not follow Oliver's lead and race toward the man she loved. But she was only doing this once, and she wanted to enjoy every second.

"Ready?" Her dad's question brushed against her ear. He held out his arm for her.

Kim threaded her hand through her father's arm. Unable to speak, she nodded.

"You made a good choice, sweetheart. Your mother and I are very proud of you." He kissed her cheek and led her through the double doors.

Kim's gaze moved over their guests. Her community gave so much of themselves to support her and Oliver, especially these last few months, as they recovered from the trauma. Her freezer had enough prepared meals that it would be many months before Kim needed to cook a dinner. But more than the practical help, she'd never forget how they stood in the gap and prayed without ceasing for Oliver's return.

Tiffany blushed again when their eyes met, but Kim didn't have time to ponder her strange appearance. Her gaze found Jackson, and everything faded. On the arm of her dad, she began the slow march toward her future.

God is a good, good Father.

## To Sweet Beginnings in Sycamore Hill

FREE: SERIES INTRODUCTION

*Sign up for Stacey's newsletter and see how it all began for the couples you love from Sycamore Hill.*

When a whistleblower speaks up, she tips the first domino of a twenty-four-hour chain reaction on the eve of Sycamore Hill's most important holiday event. A baker gets a career-making opportunity, a reporter chases the truth, a woman faces her greatest fear, and a lost child returns as the dominos continue to fall. The residents of Sycamore Hill approach a new year, and five couples celebrate sweet beginnings filled with endless possibilities in this short story sequence.

## OWEN AND GLORIA: THURSDAY 2:00 P.M.

**Sycamore Hill's prodigal daughter returns, shaking up the small town, righting a wrong, and finding the faith and family she'd lost along the way.**

Gloria hasn't returned to Sycamore Hill since her university declared her guilty of cheating. She'd lost more than her home that day; she'd lost her faith in humanity. But when a questionable drug study with ties to the university endangers the residents of a Sycamore Hill ministry, Gloria can no longer remain quiet. She returns to town, and Owen—the town's unmarried pastor and the only person who believed in her innocence—helps her to finally and truly come home.

## ETHAN AND KATHRYN: THURSDAY 11:59 P.M.

**When you mix two former sweethearts, one missing recipe, and a dash of secrecy, what do you get? A recipe for romance!**

Kathryn took something that belongs to Ethan. Correction. It belongs to his family. Taking it back isn't stealing, and letting himself into Kathryn's house to get it is not breaking and entering if he has a key. However, Kathryn's not a thief. She'd found Ethan's recipe. But when her actions threaten to spoil Ethan's bakery, they whip up a solution on Kathryn's internet morning show, Sycamore Hill at Sunrise.

## BEN AND EMMA: FRIDAY 3:00 A.M.

**God closes a door, but He opens a skylight, entwining Ben and Emma's future in the twilight hours of a winter's eve.**

Nursing school made dating impossible for Emma, and now that she finally has time to think about a relationship, the pickings are slim, especially in a small town like Sycamore Hill. She's begun petitioning the Lord to drop Mr. Right into her life, ideally before a black-tie gala fundraiser. She can't bear the idea of attending alone —again.

When Ben—a local reporter—chases the scoop of a lifetime, he falls painfully into Emma's kitchen. With a whistleblower about to rip the lid off a scandal that'll put the small town on the map, Ben needs Emma's help to follow the career-making lead and protect the residents of Sycamore Hill.

## ELI AND MEG: FRIDAY 7:35 A.M.

**At some point, a girl has to stop running and fight.**

**Eli is willing to help Meg, but how can he fight an unknown enemy?**

Eli and Meg trained together every morning to prepare for an annual road race. When Meg is uncharacteristically late on race day, Eli knows in his gut that something is wrong. He finds Meg facing her greatest fear, and Eli thrusts himself between her and an aggressive animal. However, when Meg passes up an opportunity to escape to safety, he realizes no one in Sycamore Hill really knows Meg at all.

## JACKSON AND KIM: FRIDAY, 6:00 P.M. AND SATURDAY MORNING

**Kim didn't want to like her ex's twin brother, but how could she not like the man returning her abducted son?**

Kim doesn't have the mental headspace to host the black-tie gala on the eve of her abducted son's homecoming, but she must. As she grapples with conflicting emotions about the morning reunion, she clings to the message of Christmas: God with us.

Returning his nephew to Canada destroyed Jackson's relationship with his twin brother. And after all his brother had put Kim through, she might not welcome the continued presence of Jackson or his parents in Sycamore Hill. Sorting out the legalities won't be easy, but the right thing rarely is. Jackson will do what is right, whatever the personal cost, trusting the message of the season.

*Sign up for Stacey's newsletter and read for free! If you're already subscribed, input the email you subscribed with and you'll be able to download the ebook.*

## A Sycamore Secret

BOOK 5

Ethan's custom coffee blend pairs with Kathryn's social media following in A Sycamore Secret, brewing a latte of trouble when Tiff returns to Sycamore Hill. Read the stunning conclusion to the Sycamore Hill series.

## CHAPTER ONE - A SYCAMORE SECRET

"Did you get that?" Kathryn Withers broke character, but she didn't move from where she stood. She didn't want to change positions until she knew Gloria had captured the clip.

Gloria Sycamore lowered the camera and peered at its digital screen. "I think so." She scrunched her face. "Want to see?" She offered Kathryn the device.

Kathryn reversed the footage. "I love the way you caught the sun glinting off the gilded sign for *The Muffin Man*, and still managed to angle the shot so there's no glare on the front display window. And you kept me front and centre." Heat rose to Kathryn's face at how vain that probably sounded. "You're really good at this. Ethan's going to love it."

Every so often, Kathryn gave her boyfriend's shop a shout-out on her show. A little free PR came with the territory of dating an influencer. Ethan was adding a coffee roasting lab to his bakery to set himself apart from the coffee chains opening store fronts in Sycamore Hill. The chains might pour big bucks into their businesses, but *The Muffin Man* was the only place that roasted fresh beans onsite. "If you weren't already employed, I'd offer you a job." A volunteer job, of course, because internet T.V. didn't pay beans.

Not even coffee beans.

Gloria grinned. "Does that mean we can go inside?

I'm starving and smelling all those baked goods and coffee is killing me."

"Absolutely. My treat." Buying Gloria a cup of the best coffee blend in town was the least she could do. Especially since she couldn't afford to pay her friend.

Getting *Sycamore Hill at Sunrise* up and running required long hours and a heart devoted to the craft. It was the cost of fame. Being admired was all Kathryn ever wanted, but after years producing the show, even she had to confess the spotlight had lost its brilliance. Not that she'd admit that to anyone. To the rest of the world, she was Kathryn Withers, internet sensation and social media influencer. But inside, she would always be Kathy, a little girl, looking for the place she fit in.

"I think Meg's working." Their friend worked part time for Ethan to help pay for university. "She said she had news for us."

"Another good reason to call it a wrap." They had more than enough footage. Kathryn tended to over-record and then ruthlessly cut. She meticulously produced each minute of the show. That was the only way to ensure she delivered what her audience expected—a little self-depreciating humor, a pretty face, and up-to-date local news. In other words, gossip, but the harmless kind that didn't hurt anyone. Kathryn could never be cruel.

As they packed the equipment into protective cases, Gloria chatted about the upcoming church picnic and the new recipe she was trying for the potluck.

"No sushi?"

A laugh bubbled out of Gloria. "I learned my lesson the last time. I'm sticking to noodles, cheese, and some sort of creamy condensed soup."

Kathryn admired Gloria. Coming home to Sycamore Hill hadn't been easy, and finding her place in the community as Pastor Owen's bride was even harder. But worthwhile things were difficult, and they rarely played out the way a person expected. Kathryn's gaze drifted over her film equipment. Kathryn achieved what she'd always thought she wanted—the spotlight, admiration, and success. But she never expected it to be so exhausting or unfulfilling.

Kathryn slung the camera bag over her shoulder and followed Gloria through the bakery door. A string of bells announced their arrival.

Meg looked up from behind the cash register. "Grab a table. I'll bring you coffees in a minute," she said, before handing a customer his change.

Kathryn wove through the tiny tables for two and four people, choosing one with a clear line of sight into the kitchen. Most customers came for the coffee, but Kathryn came for her Muffin Man. She smiled at the sight of him rocking the apron she'd given him, with *Do you know the Muffin Man?* silk-screened on it. At first, she'd worried adding the phrase had been a mistake since his dad used to tease Ethan by dancing around him and singing that song. His dad also called him Betty Crocker, but they'd put that behind them. His dad apologized over a year ago for how he tormented Ethan for choosing a career in baking.

A hairnet tamed Ethan's dark hair. Kathryn had always loved the slight wave in it and how he kept it just long enough that she could thread her fingers through it at the nape.

Meg clunked two mugs onto the table and poured coffee from the pot she carried in her other hand. "This is Ethan's latest blend. You'll appreciate its notes of vanilla and creamy body."

"Kathryn's appreciating a different kind of body." Gloria looked pointedly toward the kitchen.

Meg snickered. "I see the lady prefers a full-bodied darker roast. Perhaps the title of Mrs. Muffin Man is in the near future?"

Kathryn quickly sipped her coffee to mask the scorching in her cheeks. Marriage looked good on her friends. Meg and Eli had married first. Gloria and Owen wed just last month in a beautiful May ceremony, beating their friends Kim and Jackson to the altar by a week. Emma and Ben's wedding was this fall. One by one, all her friends had made their relationships official.

Except her.

The cheese stands alone.

Kathryn cut her gaze back to Ethan. She'd never felt pressure to tie the knot, but now she and Ethan were the only ones left unhitched. The coffee turned bitter in her mouth—the taste uncomfortably similar to that of never being the chosen wife in the grade school game, The

Farmer in the Dell. She was always the cheese— smelly, ordinary, and lonely. But even Scripture said there were all sorts of dishes and bowls in the kitchen. Some were made of precious metals, others of wood and clay. Some were saved for special occasions, others for ordinary use.

Ethan lifted his face and their gazes met. His expression lit up, and she felt anything but ordinary. He hurried to their table and dropped a kiss on her forehead. "All done filming?"

"I think so. And if I wasn't, I'm done anyway." Kathryn tugged off her magnetic false eyelashes. "I need to get this film makeup off."

Ethan set a muffin in front of her and grazed her cheek with the back of his fingers. "You're gorgeous au naturel."

Meg elbowed Gloria. "That's service with a smile."

Gloria smirked. "More than a smile."

Even though she'd known Ethan since they were kids at summer camp, Kathryn's insides still tingled when he looked at her like that. She felt like the tastiest item on his menu. Maybe her farmer would pick a wife after all? Kathryn dug in her shoulder bag for a facial wipe and avoided making eye contact with her friends. She swiped the cleansing tissue across her forehead. "Social media is a cruel and unforgiving employer."

"No kidding," Meg snorted. "Did you hear about that travel writer that was complaining about how hard it is to maintain a healthy lifestyle while traveling?"

"Is that the guy from *Eating on the Road*?"

Of course, Ethan knew who it was that Meg referenced. He followed a ton of foodies on social media.

Meg nodded. "He partnered with the nutritionist from *Killing Carbs.* They created easy recipes that only required the supplies found in a standard hotel room."

Kathryn's gut flipped. She'd seen that in her news feed. Something about steaming a chicken breast using a coffee maker.

Gloria giggled as she pulled it up on her phone. "*#EatingRoadKill* is trending. People are posting images of the failed recipes."

Kathryn cringed. Hijacked hashtags were the worst. There was no way for a content creator to control it once it went viral. Her friends didn't understand.

Big brands trended for ridiculous missteps and poorly crafted posts. There were no backsies on the internet. Some people might say all publicity is good publicity, but having your life's work rebranded as *Eating Road Kill* by feverish followers couldn't be good. One negative connection like that could sink Kathryn, and everything she worked for would be gone.

"Kathryn?"

Ethan touched her arm, and she jerked. By her friends' stares, she realized she'd missed something.

"Are you okay?"

"Better than okay." Kathryn beamed her ray of artificial sunshine. It's what everyone expected from her. Anything less and she might as well axe her show herself.

"But I'm afraid I missed what you said. My mind..." She fluttered her hand.

Meg's hand dropped and rested protectively across her middle.

Kathryn's heart skipped. "Are you?" Her gaze lowered to Meg's belly before darting to Gloria, who was nodding. "Are you pregnant?"

"Yes!" Meg squealed.

Kathryn shot to her feet and threw her arms around her friend. "That's wonderful!"

Outwardly, Kathryn did all the right things. She smiled, laughed, and wiped the corners of her damp eyes. But inside, another narrative played. If Meg was pregnant, it wouldn't be long before the others caught baby fever and their social circle moved from coffee shops to playgrounds. Her gut quivered, but with none of the earlier delightful notes. This time, the sourness sank deep. Like the last kid waiting to be picked, dread clawed up her spine. The cheese stood alone, indeed.

The bell over the door jingled.

"Tiff?" Gloria's tone was sharper than the social media comments on Eating Road Kill. And who could blame her after the way Tiff framed Gloria and endangered the residents of Life House.

Tiff hovered in the doorway, twisting her hands.

*What is she doing here?* Kathryn's inner quaking morphed into waves.

A hesitant smile replaced Tiff's usual confident grin. She directed her smile at Kathryn, not Gloria.

Plausible reasons for her and Tiff knowing each other failed to gel. All Kathryn could think of was the truth, and the truth was not an option. She dipped her head.

The feet on Gloria's chair scraped as she pushed to her feet. Meg stepped closer to Gloria and pulled her into a side hug before addressing Tiff. "What are you doing here?"

Kathryn peeked. Tiff rolled her lips between her teeth.

No one watched Kathryn except Tiff.

Kathryn gave her head a small shake.

Tiff deflated. Her shoulders rounded, and her eyes dulled as she shifted her gaze from Kathryn to Gloria.

Kathryn's chest squeezed. It wasn't her fault she wasn't ready. Tiff just showed up. That wasn't the plan. What good was a plan if a person didn't stick to it? Kathryn needed time to prepare. Tiff was supposed to give Kathryn a heads up. She was supposed to tell her when and where it would go down, not just *appear*. Sure, Kathryn hadn't answered Tiff's recent email because she didn't know how, but that didn't mean Tiff could just arrive.

Okay. *Emails*. Plural. There wasn't just one. And Kathryn did reply. She just didn't answer the part about Tiff coming to Sycamore Hill because that could ruin everything Kathryn had built.

"I'm here to explain," Tiff said. What she needed to explain didn't need clarifying. Everyone in Sycamore Hill knew Tiff Duthie's scheming had cost Gloria her degree.

Between that and the fact Meg benefited from the ministry of Life House, Tiff was lucky this welcome wagon didn't run over her.

A muscle twitched in Gloria's jaw. "I'm not interested."

Tiff's gaze darted to Kathryn before bouncing back to Gloria. But not before Kathryn saw the disappointment in it. Tiff would never disclose how she and Kathryn met. It would violate the code, which meant Kathryn's secret was safe.

For now.

Kathryn dampened her lips. How was she going to play this?

"I saw you at Kim's wedding," Meg said, buying Kathryn more time to think. Meg folded her arms. "Crashing a wedding. Uncool."

Tiff blinked rapidly and averted her eyes. She needed support. But that wasn't Kathryn's fault. There were tons of other people she could call on after she left The Muffin Man. It didn't have to be Kathryn. That had to be a conflict of interest. *Hi-ho, the derry-o*, Kathryn didn't want Tiff to choose her. She'd rather stand alone.

Kathryn stared at The Muffin Man's window display. She blinked until the pressure behind her eyes lessened. Helping Tiff wasn't optional. She knew that she'd help. But not until she figured out how to do it without destroying the life she'd built.

Kathryn's sandcastle was slipping through her

fingers. She needed more time. She stood. "Gloria, we should film the next segment."

Gloria nodded, looking just as eager as Kathryn felt to get away. Only, Gloria's thankful expression heaped guilt upon guilt. Gloria thought she was helping her leave with dignity, but Kathryn was using her. She was the one who needed to escape.

"Yes." Gloria slung her purse strap over her shoulder. "Let's go."

Kathryn threw a small smile to Ethan, who nodded encouragingly. He thought she was protecting Gloria, too. Shame heated her cheeks as she followed her friend. She held her breath until the bells over the door jingled as it swung closed behind them. Guilt crushed her chest.

When a fellow addict reached out, you didn't walk away.

*His custom coffee blend, paired with her social media following, brews a latte of trouble.*

When the Audience Favorite Awards include Kathryn Withers's independent web show as a finalist, the internet trolls slither out from under their bridges. Kathryn livestreams daily, growing her following and improving her chances of winning, but trending on social media backfires. The generated buzz connects the arrival of an unwelcome guest in Sycamore Hill to a shameful secret in Kathryn's past. A secret she'd do *almost* anything to keep hidden.

Ethan Roberts invested every penny in expanding his bakery, The Muffin Man, to include on-site coffee roasting. When Kathryn streams from his location, the increased visibility boosts his confidence that everything he has ever wanted is at his fingertips. But the frenzied online comments and lingering paparazzi prove that mixing a tenacious morning show host, an entrepreneurial baker, and a decade-old secret only percolates trouble.

**A Sycamore Secret is filled to the brim with small-town charm, a faith-filled community, and a slow-roasted romance perfectly brewed to a sweet and smooth finish.**

*The Sycamore*
*Standoff*
BOOK 1

Eli and Meg's story continues in The Sycamore Standoff, where Meg wants independence and Eli wants her affections. They'll have to face her past for any chance of a future.

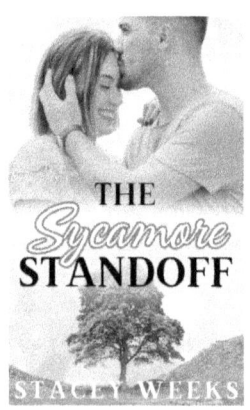

*A man with a plan. A woman with a past. A thorny adventure called love.*

**Welcome to Sycamore Hill, where hearts mend, redemption is within reach, and love's blossoms endure even the harshest storms.**

Landscape Architect Meg Gilmore's past resurfaces, threatening the harmony she's fought to cultivate. She's forced to confront the powerful family of Eli Martin, a friend she thought she could trust. With a 250-year-old tree—the very heart of Sycamore Hill—at stake, Meg and Eli's goals intertwine. For now.

Eli's roots run as deep as the ancient tree, and his noble intentions clash with familial expectations. He tries to help Meg—the first woman to see beyond his wealth and status—but only jeopardizes their future. Will Eli and Meg find their way out of the weeds and let love bloom, or will their secrets tear them apart?

**Explore themes of trust, forgiveness, community, and the resilience of love in this stirring tale of redemption. Fans of Karen Kingsbury and Deborah Raney will love The Sycamore Standoff. Buy now before the price changes!**

## His Sycamore
## Sweetheart

BOOK 2

Gloria and Owen's story continues in His Sycamore Sweetheart, where Gloria is willing to do anything to salvage her reputation except the one thing the community demands.

*She wants acceptance. He wants approval. They get a wardrobe malfunction, confusion, and a church scandal.*

Gloria Sycamore returns to Sycamore Hill and takes on the ultimate challenge: regaining the town's trust while juggling the hilarious and downright chaotic pleasure of dating their beloved minister. Under the watchful eyes of the public, privacy is a luxury, and every decision she makes is open for debate.

Pastor Owen finds himself stuck between a rock and a hard pew when rumors of biblical proportions create a divine dilemma for him and Gloria. The congregation's collective eyebrows shoot higher than the church steeple as whispers reverberate through the hallowed halls. Owen struggles to balance his flock's demands with his heart's desires. Will he rise to the occasion, or will he find himself delivering sermons to an empty room?

Despite Gloria's illustrious family name and Owen's honourable character, Gloria and Owen are caught in the throes of a scandal. As the community continues to question Gloria's commitment to her faith, the town, and their treasured pastor, the pews become a battleground for an uproarious holy war.

**Hold on to your pew, don your finest church hat, and prepare for a side-splitting journey of misadventure in this delightful blend of faith and devotion topped with a whole lot of heart. A captivating romance, witty narrative, and a quirky**

collection of unforgettable characters guarantee His Sycamore Sweetheart will have you cheering for Gloria and Owen as they fumble their way to true love.

# The Sycamore Slopes

BOOK 3

Follow Ben and Emma's story in The Sycamore Slopes as they try to unite the split town before an avalanche of trouble buries them.

*When a family is torn apart, the battle lines are drawn and the fight to control Sycamore Hill heats up.*

Ben Sawyer gives the vulnerable a voice and strives to protect them, but he can't stop the avalanche of trouble descending on his nephew. His strongest opponent isn't the grumpy Grinch sowing discord in the community, but the one person he believed would always be by his side: Nurse Practitioner Emma Powles.

Emma Powles is busy in her newly established medical clinic as the fallout from sledding and skating accidents inundates her clinic. She treats the suspicious injuries of a local child and she's forced to intervene for the girl's safety. Her actions rouse traumatic memories in Ben, testing the foundation of their relationship. Will the echoes of Ben's past shatter their future?

**The Sycamore Slopes is an enthralling romance that seamlessly weaves together family drama, small-town politics, and powerful themes of resilience.**

Finding the treasure hidden in trials

*Order now!*

Do you long for the joy of complete dependence on God yet fear the cost of full surrender? Do you long for unconditional acceptance and love but fear exposing your heart? Do you long for solid peace, absolute trust, and contentment amidst alarming circumstances but fear that those circumstances might shatter your soul?

We fight God for control of our lives because we worry that

suffering will overwhelm us. We want a future free of risk, hurt, and heartbreak. But God isn't calling us to risk-free lives —He is calling us to surrender. Some of God's greatest blessings are hiding behind those parts of our lives that are most difficult to surrender.

The first edition won the Women's Journey of Faith award. The second edition of Glorious Surrender includes five personal, in-depth study times in the Word to aid in the application and understanding of Scripture.

## PRAISE FOR GLORIOUS SURRENDER

In Glorious Surrender, Stacey Weeks writes with transparency about the tension and the transformation that her role as a pastor's wife played in bringing her to the place of ultimate freedom—one who seeks God's glory above all else. She communicates with honesty about the messiness of real life in public ministry, and takes readers on a journey through raw life topics including pride, living authentically, finding true rest in the chaos, and spiritual warfare. Her passion for God's glory to preoccupy and transform everyday living accompanies every thought on every page. This book is not just for pastors' wives, it is for women wanting to take a vulnerable look at the sins and deceptions that lurk within their minds and hearts that can stall their progress toward finding true purpose. A must read!

— ANDREA THOM, AUTHOR OF

RUTH: REDEEMING THE DARKNESS
AND AMOS: COME AWAKE!

Often we sit in our seats and wonder what the life of
our pastor is like but forget that there is another
person in that relationship that must honour the
God-given calling of that man. Glorious Surrender is
more than Stacey's story; it is about God's ability to
shape any ordinary person into the image of Him.

— KEVIN MILLER, CHURCH ELDER

If you want to glorify God in everything you think,
say, and do, I recommend reading Glorious
Surrender.

— TAMI SWARTZ, BIBLICAL
COUNSELLOR

# Acknowledgments

Writing is never a one-person adventure. Despite the hours I live inside my head working on a story or book, countless others invest in the project. I would have never created Sycamore Hill without the encouragement of my writing friends in the Brantford Writers Group. Thank you, Karen, Sandy, Heather, Tara, and Deirdre for your enthusiasm and belief in me. You believed these characters had more to their stories.

Thank you to an extraordinary editor, Olivia, from LivEdits. You helped tie the threads of this story together. I look forward to our next project together.

A special thanks to the many authors who answered my questions and to Rick Ryerse for your policing expertise. All mistakes are mine.

# About the Author

Stacey is a ministry wife, mother of three teenagers, and a sipper of hot tea with honey. She loves to open the Word of God and share the hope of Christ with women. She is a multi-award-winning author, the primary home-educator of her children, and a frequent conference speaker. Her messages have been described as rich in the truths of Scripture, gospel-infused, and life-changing. Stacey has a Graduate Certificate in Women's Ministry from Heritage College and Seminary and is working toward a Graduate Certificate in Biblical Counselling.

**f** facebook.com/writerSWeeks

**X** x.com/writerSWeeks

**⊙** instagram.com/writersweeks

# You Can Make a Difference

REVIEW ONE SYCAMORE SUNDAY

Did you enjoy this book? You can make a difference. Honest reviews of books bring them to the attention of other readers. If you enjoyed this book, I would be grateful if you could spend a few minutes to leave an online review.

- Goodreads
- Bookbub